COMING OUT

BALLARAT CHARTER

LILA ROSE

Second Edition 2019

ISBN: 978-0648483519

CHAPTER ONE

A YEAR BEFORE REUNITING WITH ZARA

MATTIE

*T*he locker room was rowdy and cold. It didn't help I was staring blindly into my locker wearing only a towel. Droplets of water cascaded down my body, dripping onto the floor. A shiver raked through me responding to the frigid air. Damn, had Coach even turned on the heat? I didn't know. I knew nothing but the thoughts destroying my brain. I was a fake, an idiot, and more significantly, scared. For four years, I'd pretended to be someone I wasn't. Four years of hiding who I was from my family; four years of hurting others in my life because I was weak.

"Hey, Alexander," Peterson called, poking his head around the corner of the lockers. "Coach got a masseur and it's your turn. But watch your arse. You can just tell the guy's gay."

Once he disappeared, I banged my head against my locker.

Could Peterson, or any of the guys on the football team tell I was gay?

No.

Because I made sure no one knew.

Why?

Because I was a phoney.

I made sure they saw me with random women, drinking and, even worse, talking shit about gay people. Each time, every comment made me sick to the stomach.

But I knew how they were. They hated people like me. They picked on and taunted people like me.

However, what caused me to shut my mouth for so long, what caused me to keep to myself about liking men, was what happened three years earlier. Witnessing some meat-heads bash a guy for being gay, punching out their disgust with every hit and kick, sealed my decision to live a lie.

Bang. My head made contact with the locker.

Shit. Why am I so weak?

It wasn't like my parents wouldn't understand and support me no matter what. Heck, I knew they'd love me if I wanted to be the next Madonna in drag. Even my alpha ex-army dad, would tell me I was being stupid pretending to be someone I wasn't.

Some days, I wished my sister was still around to talk to, to confide in. But she wasn't and she couldn't be there because of yet another meat-head jerk.

Still, a small amount of worry constantly seeped in, especially worry that my sister would turn me away—she'd hate that I was gay. Though, she did have a huge heart, so I could only hope she wouldn't. I was being selfish for wanting her there. I was being selfish for wanting to load my troubles onto her when she had her own crap to deal with, and her crap was a lot worse than mine. Zara, my twenty-five-year-old sister, was on the run for her life, to save not only herself, but her daughter from the man she married when she was my age, nineteen.

So she needed to stay safe, which was also why I didn't ring or Skype with her. She'd be able to tell something was wrong and she'd come home, so I couldn't chance it. No matter how much I needed or wanted her support.

Hell, I had to man up and soon, for my own sanity. Which was why, later that night, I was heading home to tell my parents I was gay.

It was a start at least, even if it scared me.

I was sick of being weak.

"Alexander." Coach boomed my name.

"Coming," I yelled.

"Not bloody fast enough," Coach grumbled as I walked around the corner. "Good, you're still in your towel," he said, eyeing me up and down quickly. "It's your turn to take a rub-down. New system the sponsors are doin' for their players on the university team, to keep you all playing and happy." He snorted. "We'll see how long that lasts."

"Hmm." There seemed little else for me to say. It was easy to pretend the reason why I chose to play football was for my love of it and the experience. In reality, I knew better. It was a good front with the meat-head idiots.

I shrugged. The pretence wouldn't matter soon enough anyway, because I was going to quit. I planned to leave the team as soon as I came out of the closet. It'd save all the shit that'd be, no doubt, flung my way.

Opening the door a few rooms down from Coach's office, I walked in with my head hanging low. My mind was occupied on other things, until I heard, "Lie on the table, face down." My head snapped up to the owner of the sad voice and my eyes landed on the most handsome man I had ever seen. He was tall. My head tilted a little to look up at him and then my eyes drifted down to see his upper arms showing he held muscle, enough to make me want to see what was under his white tee. His hair was darker than my brown, short and unruly hair. His moss green eyes glared at me.

Shit. My dick behind the flimsy towel twitched.

"Come on, I don't have all day."

How many men had he touched already? How many men did he still have to touch?

Thinking about it pissed me off. My nostrils flared, my body flushed in anger and I found myself clenching my jaw.

I wanted to be the only one who he had his hands on. I wanted to…yeah, I *wanted* him. A shudder ran through my body imagining his hands on me. I couldn't wait, the sooner the better, especially if my dick continued to grow hard.

A snort touched my ears. I looked to his face as I approached the table. His nose twitched, his eyes were hard, like he was angry at me. Also within his eyes, I saw they held a certain amount of hurt.

I could only assume he mistook the shudder for disgust or annoyance when I felt the exact opposite. I was turned on and the locker room was the worst place to be aroused.

"I…" I started, only I didn't know what to say. I couldn't say anything. Instead, I flattened my sore body onto the table. My face rested in the hole at the end, immediately making me think of slipping into another hole.

Jesus. I needed to get laid. My thoughts were going to get me in trouble.

When his hands touched my skin, I jumped, and as soon as his warm hands bit into my muscles, I clamped my top teeth down on my bottom lip to keep from moaning.

I needed to say something, anything.

"You…"

Fuck it. That was obviously the best I could do.

"Yes, I'm gay, but don't worry your pretty little head over it. You don't do anything for me." While his voice contained anger, it sounded deflated.

Wait.

He thought I was pretty?

Handsome I could stand.

But pretty?

Wait.

He also said I didn't do anything for him.

Damn.

"I-I don't care." I clenched my hands as his magical fingers worked my back. Would it be ridiculous if I purred?

Christ, I sounded like my sister. She always thought and voiced strange stuff.

The man snorted and dug in his hands harder into my lower back.

Goddamn, go lower. LOWER.

"What—you don't care that you don't do anything for me, or that I'm gay?"

Great. If I said yes to both then he'd know I was...inclined his way. If I said yes to the last, then he wouldn't suspect. Something told me I wanted to wait and shock him on a later date. The game would be fun. It'd also give me a chance to get to know him.

"The last," I answered. "What's your name?"

"Julian. Why you asking, sugar? You want to scream my name later when you're fisting your cock?"

My eyes widened at the thought, a thought that sounded mighty fine.

Instead, I scoffed. "No."

He hummed to himself. I would have loved to have known what he was thinking. "What's your name?" he asked.

5

"Matthew," I said as he worked my back. Was he going to go low or not?

My question was answered moments later when his hands suddenly left me and landed on my upper thighs. He squeezed them. I closed my eyes and mouthed, *Fuck.*

"Do you like my hands on you, Mattie?" he drawled, running his hands slowly up and down the back of my legs, just inches shy of my lower arse cheeks.

Please keep going, my dick sang.

What am I doing? my mind thought.

But shit, I knew it was a test, either that or he was looking to get fired on his first day.

So I played his game. "Sure, you're good at what you do."

He growled low. I smirked.

"The other guys were running from the room by now," he said.

Shrugging, I said, "Why do you want to get fired?"

He stopped, his hands fell away, and I turned to see his surprised face. Surprised I had figured him out maybe.

Shit, he was so good-looking. I wanted to do so many things to him. I wanted to roll over and show him my erection to see his reaction. I wanted to run my hands over him, like he had me, only I would have taken it further.

However, I did none of those. I couldn't and it annoyed me, pissed me off. I sat up from the table, my back to him and I secured the towel firmly around my waist. I glanced over my shoulder and said, "Why don't you just leave?"

I knew it sounded harsh and I knew he'd take it the wrong way. I meant why did he want to get fired? Why couldn't he just leave if he didn't like the job? Still, I didn't correct my mistake, even when I saw the pain in his eyes, and the flinch in his body when he *did* take my words the wrong way. I did nothing but stand and walk out of the room, leaving me feeling like a prick.

I knew Julian would be plaguing my mind from that day out.

AFTER I SHOWERED to get the oils from my skin, I dressed and made my way home. It was hard—pun intended—not to masturbate in the shower, thinking of Julian and his hands, but there were teammates around still.

I did think of staying until they all left. Mainly because I was worried that if Julian played the same game with all of my team mates, he could get hurt, and I didn't like the thought.

However, because I knew Coach was working late, I figured he also wouldn't let anything happen, so I left.

On the way home though was another story. My mind plagued me and I'd ended up turning my car around to check he was okay. I did this so many times, only to turn it back around and head for home.

Somehow, after many inner arguments, I still ended up pulling into my driveway, technically my parents' driveway, because I still lived with them. That was until I found the perfect place for myself. I'd saved and was still saving enough money with my casual job at the local real estate office that I hoped I would soon find the right house to move to.

After I dropped the 'gay' bomb, I would need my own place so much more. My mum could be...a lot to handle sometimes, always questioning when I would settle down, when I would bring home the 'right' girls instead of the sluts I was shagging. *Her words, not mine.*

Stepping into the cool night air pulled a shiver from me. I shouldered my backpack and made my way to the front door when it opened. I found a smiling Mum standing in the doorway.

"Let me guess, you were just skyping Zara?" I asked as I kissed her cheek, and slipped in past her.

Mum clapped her hands and gleefully said, "Yes, and I saw Maya. She is such a cutie. Then I spoke with Deanna. That woman sure can cuss like a sailor."

"How is everybody?" I moved my backpack to the floor near the front door and followed Mum into the kitchen where Dad was at the kitchen sink carving the roast meat. Looked like lamb.

"Don't forget to take your bag to your room before I fall over it," she said before adding, "They're all doing great. We talked about going to Melbourne one day to meet with them. Isn't that wonderful? We just need to sort a few things out—"

"Like what?" I laughed. "You're both retired." Mum was a retired nurse and Dad was an ex-army man.

Dad put the knife down and said, "Son, you know I have bowls, darts, and other shit to do. I can't just up and leave them. People would be lost without me. Then there's also all the crap your mother does."

"Crap?" Mum demanded with her hands on her hips. "Do you even know what I do these days, Rich?"

Dad rolled his eyes at Mum's dramatics. I made myself busy setting the table while they bickered to each other.

"Yes, Nancy. I know everything you do and all of it is amazing, great, super and fantastic."

"Don't patronise me or you'll be sleeping on the couch," Mum snapped as she placed the vegetables on the kitchen table.

"Drink?" I asked.

"Thank you, sweetie, I'll have a glass of wine," Mum said and then slapped Dad's hand away from the meat he was stealing.

"I carved it, woman. Beer me, boy," Dad said gruffly, then walked around the counter and placed the tray of meat on the table.

Their relationship was...strange, but full of love. I often

wondered if I would ever get to have something that precious in my life. I wanted to meet my other half, the one who would put up with my shit, like Mum does with Dad, or vice-versa.

Julian.

Laughing at my own thought, I sat down at the table. I looked to my Dad who took a swig of his beer, and I blurted, "I'm gay."

Of course, he spat his beer all over the table, his wide eyes meeting mine as the rest dribbled down his chin. He took the back of his hand up to wipe it away. I couldn't look at Mum. For some reason, I needed to hear, to see, what Dad thought or said first.

My heart beat out of my chest. My palms, lying on my thighs, sweated. I wanted to jump out of my own body, find those words I just said and shove them down my throat again. The silence was killing me.

Then he shrugged and took another sip of his beer before he said, "Don't bother me, son. As long as you're happy with what you are, with who you want to be with, it ain't got shit to do with me. I just want you happy, kid. If you like cock more than—"

"Richard," Mum yelled.

Dad chuckled. "It don't make a difference to me, Matthew. I love ya no matter."

My eyes stung. I clenched my jaw tightly together and sniffed. Shit. I never...why had I been so scared to tell them? I didn't know. I was stupid, that was the reason why.

Turning my watery eyes to Mum, I saw she was just as bad as me; her emotions were running the show. Her bottom lip trembled and then she smiled, rose from her seat, and I scooted back as she advanced on me, her hands going to my cheeks. "You're a brave, smart, handsome man. Nothing will change how much we love you."

"Mum," I choked.

She shushed me, kissed my forehead and pulled back to

stand, that was when she said, "Now, do you have a special someone you can introduce us to?"

Blushing, I thought of Julian once again. When she was seated, I answered, "No...not yet."

"Okay, well, when the time comes, we'll want to meet him. Need to make sure he'll be good enough for our boy."

Jeesh. That was something I wasn't looking forward to. Mum would no doubt embarrass me by asking inappropriate things.

For example, the next words out of her mouth, "Do you take or give?"

"Nancy," Dad barked. "Jesus Christ, woman."

Mum rolled her eyes. "I'm just curious."

"Mum, it's not something to discuss at dinner...or ever."

She sighed. "Fine. Now get some grub into you."

CHAPTER TWO

JULIAN

*S*tupid, stunning man. Why couldn't he have been like the other dickheads in the locker room? Why was *Mattie* willing to remain on the table and have *me* touch him when he knew I was gay...when he knew I was teasing him to try to get fired?

Maybe *he* was gay?

No, I didn't see it. I didn't get the vibe. He was a fucking football guy.

A pig, an idiot like most of them.

Though, he seemed different.

Who was I kidding; those types of guys were all the same.

I was so goddamn, spanking annoyed that none of them tattled on me to their supervisor. How was a man on the edge, like me, supposed to get fired?

Snorting, I exited my car and started for my apartment building. I should have known they wouldn't have said anything. They wouldn't want the other players knowing the gay guy...or rather, the smoking hot gay guy was rubbing them the wrong way. They wouldn't want to be teased by the other dickwads.

My plan fucking failed completely.

"Julian baby, how you doing?" I looked up the stairs and found my neighbour, Melissa, coming out of her place.

"Hey, sexy lady, I'm doing good. Could be better if I had a hot member warming my arse tonight." She giggled. "What are you up to, girl?" I asked, coming to a stop right in front of her where she threw herself at me for a hug.

"Going out for a drink, feel like tagging along?"

"Babycakes, I'd love to, but I'm buggered. Maybe another night," I said, placing a kiss on her cheek and moving across the hall to my apartment door.

"I'll take you up on that, mister. Next weekend, I want your beautiful face out with me. We'll get sloshed, pick up guys, and fuck them silly."

"Aw, sweetcheeks, sounds like a perfect plan. I haven't had my dick sucked in a long time. I'm a man in need of some lovin' from a hot piece of meat."

There was a gasp behind me. Melissa and I both spun to see who it came from and I found my parents standing at the top of the stairs.

Turning back to my door, I banged my head against it. Fuck. That was all I needed.

"Julian?" Melissa's voice was quiet, the tremor in it told me she was scared. Still, her glare indicated her annoyance that my parents had shown up.

Looking over my shoulder, I said, "It's okay. I'll be fine."

I'd lived in the apartment building for two years now, so Melissa knew my parents. She hated them, just like I did. She also knew I was in deep shit.

"J-man," Melissa uttered.

Shaking my head, I unlocked my door and pushed it open. "I'll be fine. Have a good night out, Melissa." My voice was hard, cold and wasn't my own. I could never act myself in front of my parents. They hated it. Hated me and the way I was.

Walking into my living room, I left the front door open, knowing my parents would follow. Dad wouldn't let me get away with how I just spoke, and soon enough, all the warmth from the room evaporated. Meaning my parents had just entered, bringing their cold hearts with them.

"Would you like a coffee?" I asked and headed to the kitchen. I heard the front door being slammed shut behind me and I cringed. Then I hated myself for cringing.

Fuck's sake. I was a thirty-six-year-old man and I was still scared of my parents.

Okay, that was a lie. My mum, I couldn't give two hoots about, like she did with me. However, my dear old dad was another story. I was petrified of him and he knew it. He loved it and thrived on it.

"Get in here, Julian," Dad yelled.

For a moment, as I braced my hands on the kitchen bench and closed my eyes bowing my head, I wished I could change how I was. I wished I wasn't so…gay.

And I wished I wasn't born to those two people out in my living room.

Still, no amount of wishing changed any of it.

Taking a deep breath, I opened my eyes, turned and started for the living room. When I walked in, I saw Mum by the door with her hands in front of her, wringing them together. She looked bored, and…worried.

Dad was further in the living room and as soon as I entered, he started for me. I knew not to back up; he enjoyed the chase too much. So I stopped and stood still, waiting for what was to come.

13

"What in the fuck do you think you were doing out there in the hall?" he demanded. Spittle flew from his mouth onto my face.

"I was talking," I said plainly. Nothing like the way I usually talked, like the way I liked to talk…when I was my true self, the way I wanted to be.

"Do you always talk like a little girl? You sounded disgusting." He sneered.

"I'm sorry you felt that way."

"You're sorry…no, I'm sorry that I have a son that's fucking putrid. You will not speak like that again. You will not disgrace me like that ever again. Do you hear me, Julian?"

Rolling my eyes, I replied, "Yes, Dad."

Shit, fuck, shit.

He saw the eye roll.

I knew he saw it when his fist collided with my eye.

Staggering back with my hands over my face, I heard Mum snort.

Another fist landed to my stomach. I doubled over.

"I hate what you are. So many days I wished I had a *real* son. A son who I'd be proud of. Instead, I'm stuck with a faggot like you."

"Then leave me alone. Have nothing to do with me. I don't care. I didn't want that job anyway. Why did you do that to me?"

He scoffed as Mum walked up to me and slapped me across my upturned face. Standing straighter, I stepped away from her. How could I have thought she'd be worried for my own sake? That would never happen.

"You will not talk to your father like that. We have been nothing but good to you after everything *you* have done to us. You shame us all the time, Julian. But you won't any longer; I won't have it. You will stay in that job, Julian. You will do as you are told or else—"

"You'll go to your grandfather's," Dad said, interrupting Mum.

Laughing, I said, "You can't do that, Dad. I'm thirty-fucking-six. I don't have to do anything you say."

He smiled then and there was nothing nice about it. "You don't do as we say, Julian, then we'll send your cousin, Monica, to your grandfather's."

My eyes widened. "You wouldn't." I choked back my bile, my hand going over my mouth. "You can't. Aunt Flo won't let that happen."

Oh, God. Monica was only fourteen. If they had any sway whatsoever in doing what they said, then Monica's life would be changed forever.

After all, they had done the same to me when I was only twelve. When I returned home, I was different, I wasn't the same boy I had been.

"It would have nothing to do with your aunt. She wouldn't have a choice, especially when I've been the one to keep my brother financially stable. My brother would do as I said or else he would lose any money he was getting from me, and you know he won't let that happen...no matter what."

He wouldn't either. He was under my father's thumb like many people.

Hell, like I was.

"You'd really send a fourteen-year-old girl to a molester?"

Mum shook her head and smiled. "That's only what you say, Julian."

Yes, they'd never believed their twelve-year-old son when he came home from his trip, from the devil himself, and told them his own grandfather had done things to him no other man should have.

"You both make me sick," I whispered.

"I guess the feeling is mutual." Dad chuckled. "Now, you *will* stay in that job and you *will* stop acting like a little crazy girl, or your cousin will be seeing your favourite person very soon. Do you understand me, Julian?"

"I'm not deaf, Daddy dearest."

I shouldn't have, but I was tired. I was upset and angry.

A lesson of never talking back like that to my father was taught to me a long time ago, which was why I expected his next move. His fist jutted my jaw forcefully to the side; blood spurted from my split lip.

"Watch your mouth, boy."

"He'll never learn, dear. Never." Mum sighed.

"Sometimes, I don't know why we bother, darling," Dad said, wrapping his arm around Mum's shoulders. He turned her and walked to the door. And without a goodbye, fuck you, or I hope you'll be okay, they left.

Crumbling to my knees, my forehead hit the floor. A sob tore through my chest.

Another thing to wish...I wished they never cared. I wished they left me alone.

But they were ruthless.

They'd rather send my beautiful, sweet cousin to the wolf so I'd tow their line. They liked control.

Now I had no choice but to do as they said.

I had to stay in a job I hated.

I had to listen to them.

To protect my cousin.

My front door opened. I drew up and scampered back on my arse, scared Dad was back to do more damage. But he wasn't.

Melissa's cry of concern hit my ears when she spotted me bruised and bloodied on the floor. I sent her a small smile and shrugged.

"I love having my parents come for a visit."

"Julian," she whispered, her hand going over her heart as she made her way over to me.

"Why aren't you out shagging some hottie? I'd go with you now, but I don't think I'm all that appealing at the moment." I tried for a laugh.

"Don't do that. Be yourself, but don't joke about this," she scolded.

Yeah, right. Being myself was what got me the fist to the eye in the first place. But I didn't tell her that.

"Why do you let them in?" she asked as she helped me to stand.

"Pfft, I have no choice apparently, sweetcheeks. You know that," I said.

Melissa knew what my parents were like; she knew they cared about nothing but what people thought of them or who they could control. They liked money and power, and they had it. Melissa also knew what the visits from my parents were like… that was only in the last six months though. Usually, they called for me to go to their place. However, lately, because I skipped those sweet, caring meetings, they came for me. Yeah, Melissa knew that every time they came, trouble came with them.

Trouble in a way that I'd end up hurt.

She'd usually hear the yelling and things being thrown around.

Only that time, they didn't throw anything, which surprised me. They liked to wreck my things.

After they left, Melissa was the one who came over to check on me. The first time she saw me she wanted to call the police. I wouldn't let her, of course. If they knew she was getting involved, they'd be pissed and Melissa would soon find herself in debt or worse.

"It can't keep happening, Julian."

"Leave it alone, Mel. Please," I begged, moved my arm from

17

her shoulders and went to the fridge. There, I grabbed a bag of frozen peas and placed them against my aching face.

"I hate it, J-man. I really hate seeing you like this."

"Come on, now, the bruises and cuts bring all the boys to my yard. They think it's hot."

"Why do you do that? You make a joke about it, but I can see what it does to you. I can see the light in your eyes fade away every fucking time they've been here, and it lasts at least a week after their goddamn visit."

Tears welled in my eyes. "I joke, baby. It's who I am. I joke to hide many things, but I joke because I want to, I like to, and because they hate it. They hate who I am, how I act, so I do it to defy them in a way."

Her own eyes misted. "Okay, honey. Okay, joke away." She smiled and then walked over to hug me. When I winced, after her arm hit my stomach, she pulled back and glared. She lifted my tee up and I watched her eyes spring wide when she saw my already purple stomach.

"Fine. Fucking fine. You joke, doesn't mean I have to. Instead, I'll fucking…" She took a step back and screamed. Her hands went to her waist and she glared at my stomach once she stopped. "That stupid, motherfucking bastard. How dare he do this to his own son. I'll cut him. I'll go there and fuck him up. I swear to Christ, Julian. If he comes near you again, I will go ninja crazy woman on his arse and then…then I'll fuck your mum up as well for standing here and doing nothing. This…fuck, fuck, fuck." She stomped her cute, small feet. "It fucking sucks."

"Calm down, She-Ra, Princess of Power. I love and spank you very much that you want to rain pain down on my arsehole parents, but this won't happen again. If my plan goes to…well, plan, then they won't have anything over me."

"What do you mean have something over you? What have

they got, Julian? If it's something on their computer, I can sneak in there and steal it back."

Her eyes told me she was serious. For someone who was five-foot nothing, slim and looked like the older version of Punky Brewster, with freckles on her nose and all, she was still one scary woman, if you got on her wrong side.

"Wow, you really would." My heart warmed. I was surprised it was so soon after my parents' visit.

"Of course, you were the best when I moved in here. In fact, you're my best friend, Julian. I've had a shit past, and done some bad things, but I don't mind starting back up for you."

"What do you mean starting back up?"

She looked uneasy then. "Oh, uh, nothing. Tell me what they have over you and I'll get it."

Sighing, I said, "It's not really something they have. It's more what they'll do if I don't do as I'm told." Placing the bag of peas on the counter, I gestured to the table. "Sit down, my little pumpkin pie, and let Aunty Julian tell you a story."

"Will it make me cry?"

"Possibly." I nodded.

"Great. You'll just have to buy me a whole box of Tim Tams then."

Chuckling, I said, "Deal, you monster."

CHAPTER THREE

MATTIE

*I*t had been a week since I last saw Julian. A week I was still my fake self in front of my team mates, work colleagues and friends. At home, things were great. My parents, God, they were amazing. If I could get my everyday life just as great, then things would be better. I wouldn't feel the need to stay hidden.

It also took me a week to find out that Julian only visited the locker rooms once a week. So I was keen to see if it was the day he'd show. We were in training season, getting ready for the games that would start in little over a month. After an hour of hard training out on the field, I headed to my locker when Coach yelled my last name. He, like the team members, never called anyone by their first name. "Alexander, you're up. Get changed and go get a rub down, son. You worked your arse off on the field today. Good job." As soon as he said that, he disappeared.

Jackson, the team quarterback, elbowed me in the ribs as he

stood next to me at his locker and said, "Yeah, Alexander, go get your rub down." He laughed like he made the funniest joke, and the others soon joined in with him.

"Hey," Peterson called from across the way. "I was just in there. You see the shiner the gay guy's got?"

"Nah," Jackson said. "Though the guy probably deserved it anyway, stupid fag." They all laughed.

Fucking idiots.

Ignoring them all, I stripped off my gear and placed a towel around my waist. I wondered if what Peterson said was true, if Julian did have a black eye, and if so, why?

Stalking off, I went straight to the door and opened it to find my answer. When I saw Julian's healing bruise around his eye, hell not only that, but he had a healing cut lip as well, my fists tightened on my towel. I wanted to hit the person who did that to him.

"What happened?" I demanded.

Julian scoffed and said, "Well, hello to you too, babycakes."

Blushing, I uttered, "Hi." Damn, I probably acted like a right tool demanding answers. But I wanted, no, I *needed* to know who did that to him so I could find the fucker and deal with him.

Never had I felt that possessive.

Never had I wanted to beat another so badly.

What was Julian doing to me?

"You want to shut the door and climb on the table for me, handsome?"

I wanted to do a lot more, but I couldn't. Instead, I sighed and shut the door. Turning, I made my way to the table and glanced quickly up at Julian's face. I was surprised but pleased to find him staring at my body, and then he went and licked his lips.

Shit, there went my dick again, as though it could feel Julian's lips and mouth upon it.

To hide my pounding cock, I jumped onto the table and lay

on my stomach. My erection rubbed against the table, wishing it was rubbing against something else.

And that something was Julian's arse.

I'd never had *that* before either. I knew I was attracted to men more than women. I knew I was gay because a man's body turned me on more than any woman's. But I'd never explored that option...meaning, I was a virgin in a sense. I'd never had a man's arse and no guy had been near mine.

Christ, just thinking of Julian entering my tight hole nearly made me come.

Once settled, with my face positioned, I took a deep breath to settle my aching cock. It started to relax until Julian's soft hands touched my back.

"Fuck," I whispered through clenched teeth.

His hands paused. "You okay?" he asked in a soft tone.

"Ah, yeah." Sure, fine, damn wonderful. If only my dick wasn't as hard as a rock.

Oh, damn. After Julian squirted more oils onto my back, he really started to work my muscles. The movement caused my body to shift slightly up and down on the table, which in turn, caused my dick to rub against the foldout table.

Jesus. If I didn't get myself under control, I'd blow all over the towel and table.

Think of something else damn it.

"Um...so are you going to tell me what happened?"

He snorted. "Poppet. The best part about that question is the fact that I don't have to tell you diddly squat."

Poppet.

He'd called me many pet names, but, for some reason, it was poppet I liked the most. Even though I loved the endearment, I hated he didn't answer my question. But he was right. He didn't have to answer if he didn't want to. I was nothing to him, nothing but an idiot football player.

"How old are you?" Julian's sudden question surprised me.

"Nineteen." Damn his hands felt good. "You?"

"God, you're nineteen?" He groaned. "How is that possible? Aren't the others older? You look older, act older."

I didn't like the sound of his voice. It was like he hated the fact I was nineteen. Shrugging, I said, "Most are older, around twenty, twenty-one. I think I'm the youngest on the team, but the Coach liked what I could do so he let me in." Why did I tell him all that?

"So, this is your first year at university?"

"Yes...are you going to answer my question?"

He didn't say anything for a moment, not until he'd moved and started working my calves. "What question?"

"How old are you?"

"Old enough to know better." His voice was sad when he spoke. I glanced over my shoulder to see he had a glare in his eyes and his lips were thinned, like he'd sucked something sour. What was he thinking and what did he mean by it?

I could see he wasn't going to answer my question, *again*. So I changed the subject. "I see you didn't get fired."

"My Watson, you are so observant. No, poppet, I didn't get fired. No one dobbed on the big, in-my-pants, gay guy."

Why did he want to leave when he applied for the job in the first place? So I asked him, "How come you went for the job if you wanted to be fired on the first day?"

He rubbed higher, just above my knees and I swear I was drooling. I'd be embarrassed if there ended up being a pile of drool on the floor.

"I didn't want the job, angel-cake. Though, it has its perks. I get to see near naked men all afternoon. I get to touch them, perv on them and tease them...now, if only you all liked everything I said."

I do.

What I didn't like was the fact he enjoyed touching, teasing and perving on *all* of the team. It left me feeling deflated, if only my cock got the message.

"I still don't get it. Why go to the interview for *this* job if you didn't want it?"

His hands stilled on my upper thighs and then fell away. The next second, I felt a slap to my arse. I jumped and my dick perked up even more, but it was sorely disappointed when Julian said, "We're done here. I have to get moving, I have two others to get my hands on."

Lifting my head, I looked to the clock on the far wall. "We still have ten minutes left."

"Yeah? Well, pookie, I'm not a fan of all the questions. So we'll skip the next ten. Come on, up and at 'em."

"What if I keep my mouth shut, will you keep going then?" Because, apparently, I liked to torture myself, especially my pecker.

"Fine, but no more questions. Let me just worship your body."

Yes, please.

"Nothing seems to faze you, the way I talk I mean," he uttered and the confusion in his voice was present.

No, nothing bothered me. He could do anything to me. I let out a deranged chuckle and said, "Nope, it doesn't bother me."

"Right." I thought that would have been the end of chatting. I was wrong. "Why are you so different than the rest, Matthew Alexander? The others tell me to shut the fuck up...but you, you like to talk to me. You want to know things about me. Why?"

Shit. Shit. Shit.

I didn't know the guys didn't talk to him.

"What, so it's okay for you to ask questions about me, but not for me to ask them about you, Julian?"

His light, sweet chuckle filled the room. "Touché, Mattie, touché."

For the final seven minutes, we were silent. Though, if my dick could talk, it would be yelling for attention. Instead, Julian worked my muscles like a pro, rubbing all the aches and stress away for the entire half an hour with him.

Once Julian stepped away, I sat up and secured the towel around my waist, using the edge of my hand to hold down my erection. I glanced at Julian, his eyes travelled my body. Worried he'd see I was hard, I quickly jumped off the table and made my way to the door.

"Till next time, poppet," he called.

At the door, I looked over my shoulder and sent Julian a small smile. He drew in a deep breath, his eyes on my mouth. "See you next week, Julian, with new questions."

He rolled his eyes at me, but I saw the smile lighting his face. "We'll see."

With that, I opened the door and walked out of the room, fighting myself all the way to the showers to not go back and take what was supposed to be mine.

Wow. Seriously? Mine?

Shaking my head, I smiled. I really liked the thought of Julian being mine.

AFTER I SHOWERED and dressed in jeans and a hooded jumper. I walked out of the building heading to my car. *Cock-sucking damn.* A few of my team mates were loitering near my car and they had a handful of women hanging off them. I wasn't in the mood for it, but having my car right near them, I was out of options. So I stalked my way to the car.

"Yo, Alexander. Get over here," Peterson yelled.

"Nah, man, I got shit to do."

I nearly escaped as well, until Sarah Smith, local team slut came out of the shadows as I was unlocking my car door.

"Hey, sexy. You looked good in practise, good enough to eat." She slid her arm around my waist, and before I could say or do anything, she guided me over to the other players who were now all smirking at me.

Who was I kidding? I could have stopped her. I could have said something, but I didn't, because I didn't want to look any different to the other idiots on the team.

So I glided my arm around her shoulders and brought her body close to mine.

When it came to women, I wasn't a virgin. I'd lost my virginity to an old friend/ex-girlfriend. Her name was Bella. It was when we were both fourteen and didn't know what we were doing. We stayed together for three and a half years. It was her who helped me last year to figure out why I wasn't interested in sex. I'd just been doing it with the wrong type of person.

"Later, fag," Jackson suddenly called out. I caught his chin lift to someone behind me and turned both Sarah and myself to see Julian. With his shoulders slouched, and his gait fast, he headed to his car.

"Hey, fag, you better watch those hands of yours, wouldn't want them broken." Jackson taunted.

And because I was an idiot.

Because I was a fake.

When the others laughed. I chuckled out a false chuckle with them.

Only when I did, I looked over to see if Julian had noticed. Our eyes met. In them, I saw pain. My mouth snapped shut and I hoped to Christ he saw regret in my eyes before he got into his vehicle.

Stupid. Stupid fool.

That was all I was. No, I was worse than that. I was one of them. I was a meat-head bigot. Though, I couldn't say they were all bad. Some were good guys. They weren't weak like me. If they didn't like something, they said it.

"Jackson, don't be a dick," Lions growled. "Bunch of fucking kids," he said and walked off.

"What's up his arse?" Peterson asked.

Jackson snorted. "Maybe the fag guy's dick."

They laughed once again. Only that time, I didn't.

"Hey, you okay?" Sarah asked, her hand lying across my chest.

A nod. "Yeah, fine, but I have to get home. Some family shit." I removed my arm and stepped away, walking to my car. "Later," I called over my shoulder. However, I wished I didn't. I wished I was like Lions and called them out for being fucking bastards.

I was a coward.

The drive home didn't curb my emotions. I wanted to find Julian, to apologise for what he saw, for being one of them, when deep down, I wasn't.

But I didn't, and when I walked in the house later, I saw Dad sitting in the living room chair. He took one look at me and asked what was wrong.

"Nothing," I snapped. "I just suck."

Dad snorted. "We know that now, son."

My eyes widened and a sudden burst of laughter fell from my mouth. "Jesus, Dad, I didn't mean it like that."

He chuckled. "I know, but you looked like hell coming through that door, so at least I got you to smile." He stood from his chair and added, "I'm going to get a beer, and kid, watch that mouth when you're around your mother."

Shaking my head at how sometimes my parents shocked me to the point of being stunned, I walked off toward the hall. At least there was no dull moment in the Alexander household.

In my room, my thoughts drifted back to Julian.

I had to make it up to him…one way or another. I just had to figure out how.

CHAPTER FOUR

JULIAN

*H*ow lame was I to think Mattie was different from the others. I thought he actually cared. No other jockstrap had asked how I got the black eye, one even said I probably deserved it. Not Mattie. He looked as though he wanted to beat someone up for me. So why did he turn into a wanker? The way he stood with his teammates and laughed at me, at my expense, I was gutted. Seeing him laughing sliced right into my heart.

Well, fuck him.

I wish.

No, I didn't.

Besides, the fact I was seventeen years older than him *and* he was a jerk like the rest gave me enough reason to steer clear. I had to get him off my mind. I needed to find someone else to play with.

Which was why, two days later, I was standing in a club

watching the bodies on the dance floor dry-hump each other. I also had my eagle eye out for some candy to take home that night.

"Did you hear from your aunt?" Melissa asked from beside me.

After taking a sip of my whiskey on the rocks, I looked down at her small form and shook my head. "I found out she's on a holiday with her family. Some remote area where no contact is welcome. When they get back, I'll try again."

I'd decided to go behind my parents' backs and go directly to my aunt to plead my case for my cousin's safety. I loved my aunt and she loved me. We had a close connection, even though we lived miles away and hardly spoke. She was the only one who believed me about my grandfather. At the time, she wanted to take me into her home, but of course, my father wouldn't have it.

"I hope they come back soon. If your parents come to your place again, Julian, I won't be a happy girl and they'll know about it."

If my parents were smart, which they were not, they'd stay away.

Melissa was actually being serious. I wasn't sure what her past entailed, but it was brutal and she knew how to handle herself. I had seen it one time. We'd been out clubbing—nothing new—when she stepped outside to get some fresh air. Noticing she'd been gone for a while, I went out looking for her, leaving my sparkly new toy inside, not knowing that what I saw next would have me going home alone.

When I opened the front door to exit, I didn't see her anywhere. I headed down the walkway a little and found her in an alleyway surrounded by four men. I went to run and help her —I was gay, not a pussy—until I noticed Melissa shake her head, thankfully. Because if I had gone flying to the rescue, minus my leotard, I would have had the shit beat out of me, like the four men did. It was amazing to witness a short Punky Brewster, zone into something else, where nothing mattered around her but the elimination of the four who were fucking with her.

"Not much to look at tonight," Melissa complained. We were leaning against the bar, sipping our elixir of the night when I spotted a cute, older man, wearing suit pants and a white shirt give me a smile.

"I'm not sure about that. I think I found my prey." I laughed and gestured with my head to Mr Tall and Handsome. I just hoped he was well endowed.

"Mel, Julian," was yelled from our left side. We both turned to see Cherry, an old acquaintance of ours. She giddily waved, beamed, and ran over to us. "I didn't know you two were coming tonight. It's so great to see you both here. It's been so long," she said as she hugged us. "Come on over to the booth. Mandy and Kate are there. They'd love to see you."

Looking to Melissa, I saw her shrug so I said, "Sure, butter-cake, but not for long, I need to find a nice piece of sausage for the night and I already have my eyes on one," I explained and winked at said victim, who in turn blushed, and then sent me a mega-watt smile. Cherry grabbed my hands. I reached behind me in time to take Melissa's before I was dragged to the far side of the dance floor where ten or so booth tables sat.

"Mandy, Kate, look who I found," Cherry yelled.

She pulled me to a stop beside her, in front of a booth that sat Kate, a tall, curly headed blonde, and Mandy, a chubby, black-haired beauty. "Hey, bitches." I smiled and air-kissed each woman.

"Hey all," Melissa said beside me. I glanced to see her eyes wander to another booth. I went to look until Mandy grabbed my hand and dragged me down next to her.

"Julian, I am so glad you are here. Kate and I need your help. See those guys over there, what's your take on them?"

Looking to where she was pointing, I saw a group of four men. All in jeans and different coloured tees. "My take would be to wish them all gay so I could have a go at each one of them. Alas, they were not. Though, from their relaxed posture and smiling faces, they seemed like an edible bunch, ones who would treat my girls right for the night."

"Yay," Kate yelled and clapped her hands. "Should we make the first move?"

Shaking my head, I said, "Hell to the no. Let them stalk you hooker ladies. You need to get their attention somehow." While thinking, I looked up to see Melissa in a conversation with Cherry; however, her eyes were still trained on something or someone behind me. She must have found her dipping sauce for the night.

Clicking my fingers, I announced, "I've got it. Get your sweet arses up there on the dance floor. Dance your way over to them. Do your girl thing you ladies love to do and hump each other's legs. That will get their attention."

"You are the best, babe." Kate grinned. She scooted out of the booth, and I quickly stood so Mandy could get out. They excused Cherry from her conversation with Melissa and dragged her out onto the dance floor. There they went for it, rubbing each other and grinding on each other as they danced their way across the floor.

Sitting back down, I watched when they got close to the men. It didn't take long for their eyes to find my girls. One was brave enough to make the first move, walking up to dance behind Kate. She looked over to me and gave me the thumbs up sign. I chuckled and sent her a wink.

Melissa got my attention when she sat opposite me. "I don't like it."

Puzzled, my brows drew up and I asked, "What?"

"The guy behind you at the booth, sitting with a girl; he hasn't taken his eyes off you for some reason. What I don't like is the hard stare in his eyes."

Shrugging, I said, "Twinkle-toes, I always get that look no matter where I am. He either hates me for being so awesome or wants a piece of me. But if he can't be man enough to make up his mind and either tell me to go fuck myself or tell me he wants to fuck me, then forget about it. I don't let that shit get to me so you shouldn't."

"I'm not sure it's a look of hate. He seems perplexed about something. He hates something, but I'm getting the feeling that it isn't you. I—"

"Hey."

We both looked up to see Mr Suit standing at the side of the booth, smiling shyly down at me. "Well, hello there, handsome. What can I do for you?"

Snorting, Melissa leaned back in the booth. While Mr Suit blushed and stammered out, "I-I, um, I was wondering, if, um..." He licked his lips and I knew then he wanted my lips upon his. Of course, I was more than willing to please the man.

Slowly, I stood from the booth. He didn't back up to give me room, so as soon as I was standing in front of him, our bodies rubbed against each other. The hardness at my hip indicated he was sure happy to see me. My dick perked up. He would have liked something thicker and longer to play with, but we couldn't be too picky.

"What's your name, sugar?"

"S-Steven."

He was shorter than me. I watched his eyes as they followed my mouth when I said, "Hi, Steven. My name is Julian. Want to be best of friends tonight?"

"Yes." His hands went to my hips. I placed mine on his arms, over his jacket.

"Do you want me to kiss you, Steven?" I rolled my eyes as he looked around. Probably worried what sort of scene we were making, wondering if he could get in trouble for it.

He licked his lips and nodded.

"Good answer." I smiled. Just as I was descending to touch my lips against his, he was roughly yanked away. Blinking, I stood straight and instead of having Steven in front of me, my eyes widened to find Mattie there.

"What do you think you're doing?" Mattie barked in my face, his cold eyes piercing into me.

Placing my hands on my hips, I snapped, "Well, I would have been lip locking it with that guy,"—I pointed over his shoulder to the worried Steven, though Mattie didn't turn his glare from me to look—"but then you stopped it."

"Did you not see he has a fucking wedding ring on his finger?"

Startled, I looked over Mattie's shoulder to Steven who guiltily placed his hands behind his back.

Well, damn.

"You can go now," I ordered Steven.

"But—"

Mattie turned then.

He turned, oh so slowly, to face Steven and growled, "Fuck off. *Now*." Steven visibly swallowed a big gulp of air, spun, and just about ran off.

My dick throbbed behind my jeans.

We loved Mattie's growly voice.

Once Mattie turned his glacial glare back to me, I demanded, "What are *you* doing?"

His head jutted back. "What do you mean?"

Melissa stood beside me. I glanced at her to see she was smiling as she said, "He means, why did you interrupt their little...tomfoolery?"

He opened his mouth, closed it, only to open it again to say, "He shouldn't want to...get with married men."

"Why do you care what I do?"

He blanched, took a step back and closed his eyes. Once he took a deep breath, he opened them, his eyes warmer. "I shouldn't," he uttered.

He shouldn't what? Care?

My heart thumped, smiled and screamed: *he cared.*

Why?

The man in front of me confused me more than men who wore sandals and socks together.

"Matthew, are you ready to go?" I didn't want to look away from my toy-boy's eyes. The way they searched me, the way they made me feel important was thrilling. But I did and I wished I could take back that thrill. Because a small young woman stepped up to *my* toy-boy and placed her arm around his waist.

His gaze was pulled from me. He looked down to her with devotion and smiled. "Yeah, baby, let's get out of here." His eyes landed on me for the last time and they were once again cold and unsure. "See you, Julian."

Too stunned to answer, I simply nodded and watched my dirty, erotic, dream man walk away, his arm wound around his girl's shoulders.

"Who was *that* stud?" Melissa sighed next to me.

"I...he's...oh, God." I ran a hand down my face and sat in the vacant booth.

Melissa quickly sat opposite me, waving her hand to a passing waitress. "We need drinks, make them doubles, one whiskey, one bourbon."

"Coming right up," the waitress answered.

My mind was too busy to take in anything other than the fact that Matthew Alexander, *my Mattie*, who I'd masturbated to every morning, had been in front of me. He had been there, in the club, and witnessed me nearly kissing a married man.

"He stopped it. Why would he do that? It's not like I have a conscience or anything. Hell, if a married man wants a piece of my arse, then I would let him. I'm a bad boy like that. His wife obviously isn't giving it to him how he likes it. He..." shaking my head, I leaned back.

"Julian, you're rambling. Who was that guy?"

"Kid. You mean kid. He's only nineteen."

Melissa whistled. "Seriously, the way he's built I would have pegged him to be in his mid-twenties at least. But that doesn't tell me *who* he is."

"He's on the football team I have to service, not in the way I'd prefer, once a week."

"He's a football guy?" She nodded to herself. "I can see that. He has the body for it."

I groaned. Christ, at the mention of his body I wanted to go rub one out with my hand, knowing I'd come hard doing it.

"Now it makes sense. He was watching you because he knew you."

"*He* was the one watching me?" I asked, aghast Ho no, he had seen me at my best. He saw the tart I was.

"Hell, yes. And let me tell you, he didn't like you talking to that guy."

"*Pfft.*" I snorted and rolled my eyes at her. My heart beat like a drummer was playing wildly on it.

"Seriously, he watched your every move like he wanted to take a big chunk out of you. Now I know the look he had was a 'wants to fuck you' look, not a hateful one."

Shaking my head, I said, "No way."

Nodding, Melissa said, "Yes way."

The waitress returned, and once she deposited the glasses onto the table, I knocked mine back. After Melissa paid and the waitress left, I told her all about my encounters with Matthew Alexander, aka poppet or toy-boy.

"Hmm," was her answer.

"Hmm, that's all you have to say? Hmm...is that a good hmm or a bad hmm? Do I need to tell you again? Damn it, woman, did you even listen to what I said?"

"Calm your gay-self down. Yes, I listened and the hmm was a good one...I suppose."

"You suppose, oh, well, you suppose so I can live a happy little life now. Jesus Christ on crack, give me some advice before I explode, then I can go home and wank till my heart's content over a guy, a man-boy that I can't have."

"Holy cow, that guy has really done a number on your brain."

"No shit, Sherlock," I snapped dryly.

"Okay, here are my thoughts. First, I honestly think he has a thing for you. I don't know who that woman was. To hazard a guess, I'd say they were friends. Julian, the way he watched you, the way his jaw clenched when you stood up and touched Steven was...wow, I would have crapped myself. It was as though Steven was peeing on his property."

"I think you're over exaggerating."

"Shut up, I'm talking now." She grinned. "I think you shouldn't care about his age. It's only a number after all. The way —no...hell, the *feeling* I got when the two of you were close to each other was...let's just say if I wasn't in public, I would have been twiddling with my love button because it was so sexual. No doubt about it. He wants you, even though he was pissed, jealous. And you want him, though you're frustrated." She stood from the table. "I say on your next appointment, talk to him and watch his body. You'll find he'll have a stiffy, like I know you do every time he comes near or from even talking about him." She leaned over close to me and looked at my hard cock.

I knew two things then.

Melissa was scary because she knew me too well.

And I was going to listen to her. Matthew wouldn't know what hit him come next appointment time. I just had to make sure he would be the last on my list for the day.

Actually, there were three things I knew.

Third, Thursday was a fucking long way away.

CHAPTER FIVE

MATTIE

*M*y mind was still reeling on Thursday, Julian-day, about the way I acted on the weekend. What had I been thinking? All I knew was I couldn't let Julian touch or kiss that guy. If I was to witness it, there was no telling what I would have done to that married fucking prick. My body didn't listen to my head when I told it to stop. No, it had a mind of its own, because the next thing I knew, I was pushing Bella out of her seat and striding my way to Julian, ripping that dickhead away from him and demanding to know what Julian thought he was doing.

Christ. When he looked shocked to see me standing in front of him, I wanted to pull him close and kiss the fuck out of him. Hell, I'd nearly reached up to do it. So when he turned his shock into attitude, I was thankful. Because then I was not only pissed, horny, and jealous, but I was annoyed that he didn't take notice he was about to get it on with a married man.

Still, something told me Julian wouldn't have cared if the guy was married, and that pissed me off even more.

Bella had been a godsend. She moved away a while ago, though we kept in touch. While she was in town for the night, she wanted to catch up and have a few drinks. When I acted like a tool—when I felt the idiot was touching what was mine and I didn't like it—she understood. Then she noticed me looking panicked toward the end when Julian questioned me, so she saved me. She got me out of there before I confessed my obsession with Julian.

Out the front as we walked to our cars, she squeezed my waist. "I like him for you."

"I...no...it could never work."

"Matt, have you..." she stopped and turned me toward her, her hands on my arms. "Have you experienced anything with a man yet?"

Blushing like a school boy with his first erection, I shook my head.

Her head tilted to the side and she frowned sadly at me. "Oh, Matt. Why not? I've never seen you react like that before. You didn't like that other man near Julian."

Shrugging, I said, "I don't know. I've never had the guts to try anything."

She sighed. "You need to stop being ashamed of who you are. There is nothing wrong with you, Matt. One day, you *will* see this. I just hope it's soon." We walked again, nearing our cars. "I also hope it's with that handsome guy in there."

Laughing, I shook my head. "You just don't quit."

"No, never. Not when I see the potential the two of you have." She bumped her hip against mine. "Besides, I swear he wants you as much as you want him, and I'm usually right about these things."

My heart bloomed then, at the thought of Julian wanting me

like I desperately wanted him. I couldn't think of anyone else to show me, to teach me everything. He was the first one who I really wanted to see naked, who I wanted to touch and be touched by. He was the first one I ever thought about…taking my virginity.

Damn. That sounded so corny.

Sure, there were others I'd been attracted to, that I'd fantasied about.

Only, it was never as intense as what I felt for Julian.

No one had ever consumed my mind like Julian did.

However, it still scared me. I didn't know what to do with my thoughts or how to act, and I felt like a fool for how I behaved at the club.

Which was why I was nervous, yet eager, as I waited to be called for my time to have Julian's hands on me.

I also felt like I should have run. Pretended I couldn't make the appointment. Still, I didn't. I figured I needed to walk in there like nothing happened. As though I hadn't seen him Saturday and barked in his face about that douche.

"Alexander," Coach yelled. With shaking hands, I headed around the lockers to a grumpy looking Coach. "Look, you're last up, but I need to head out." He thrust some keys at me. "Lock up after that guy's packed up. Give me the keys tomorrow," he said, then turned and walked off.

Shit. I was now there alone with the man I wanted in every way.

I nodded to myself. And nodded again.

Easy. I could do this. I could be alone with Julian.

Fine. Get it over and done with and then I could get home, eat and crash.

Without thinking of Julian and his magic hands, body, self.

Yeah, right!

Knocking on the door, I waited until I heard, "Come in."

41

Opening it, my eyes sought out the man dreams were made of, and when they landed on him, my dick jumped under the towel. He wore a simple white tee and black slacks, but they hugged his sporty form nicely. Before I had a full erection, I made my way over to the table to lie down.

"Evening, Mattie," Julian said with a smile in his voice.

"Julian," I answered, placing my face down into the hole on the table.

I heard a squirt of the bottle as he placed oil onto his hands. "How was the rest of your Saturday night?" Julian asked and then started to work on my shoulders, his fingers biting into my muscles.

"Good." *But long, since it's been four days since I've seen you. Four days of thinking of you, four days of jerking off as you played on my mind.*

Christ, I need help.

"Hmm, is this how it's going to be, short answers?"

Turning my head to meet his amused gaze, I noticed his bruises and split lip were healing. Resting my head down, I muttered, "It's how it should be."

"Really?" He laughed. "Obviously, you haven't gotten laid lately or you'd be in a better mood." His hands went down my back to my ribs as I said nothing in return.

Some time passed, long enough that the way his hands worked my body I had a full erection pressing into the table. I'd bitten my lip countless times so I wouldn't moan.

"Did you sleep with that woman?" Julian questioned, surprising me he actually asked. It also made me wonder why he was asking. Had I been on his mind as well? I didn't know how to respond, if I should lie to him or not.

However, my mouth answered for me, "No."

Julian's hands stilled on my lower back. Then I felt him shift. His heat pressed against half of my back. Then his lips gently touched down on my neck. I stiffened. At least my body did, my heart took off in a wild ride, wanting to pound out of my body.

He'd kissed my neck, a fleeting kiss, but still one.

Julian kissed my neck.

What did it mean?

My stomach clenched as nerves ate away at me.

Once he leaned away, I quickly sat up, my hands gripped the towel to me. I had an urge to run, to hide. "I-I better go," I said, not meeting his gaze. I went to jump from the table but he placed his hands quickly on my thighs, stopping me.

"Poppet?"

I didn't answer. I couldn't because I wasn't able to take my eyes away from his hands on me and concentrate on forming any coherent words that would make sense.

Julian's hands were on me.

Warming me.

Smooth, slick hands from the man who'd consumed my mind were on my thighs.

He took a step forward, his hips hitting my knees. My head snapped up to look at him, my wide panicked eyes searching his face. He looked calm, serious, with a small smile on his gorgeous lips. But when he rubbed the front of himself against my knees, my head dropped back down to take notice of the bulge behind his slacks. He was hard.

Julian was so very, very hard.

He stopped moving his hips. Still, his hands on my thighs gripped tighter and without a sane thought from myself, he separated my legs just a little, where he slipped himself between.

"W-what are you doing?" I asked in a high-pitched voice.

"Oh, nothing much." He smirked.

He shouldn't be doing that. He shouldn't be touching me, up in my personal space. I didn't like it.

Rephrase that. I was concerned by it, but my cock loved it. It bounced under the towel. I slapped my hand over it, worried Julian would notice; however, I shouldn't have moved because it was then Julian looked down.

His smile as he looked back up to me was shining. It lit up his whole handsome face. What worried me though was how he looked like the cat that got the cream.

His head tilted to the side when he asked, "Do you want a hand with that?"

Coughing, I snapped, "What?"

Stupid question.

Julian chuckled. One of his hands ran up further, sending my body into a shiver. Sweat spouted forward all over me. Under the towel now, his hand stilled just inches from my raging cock. "With this," he said and then wrapped his hand around my erection. My body jumped, my hands slammed down onto the table, trying to inch my body back, away from his hand ON MY DICK.

"I, no, you need to…" He stroked up and down. "Fuck," I moaned and closed my eyes, only to spring them back open and stammer, "S-stop, you should stop." However, my words meant nothing when my hips bucked into his hand. Wanting, needing more.

"Are you sure that's what you want, sweetheart?" Julian cooed.

No. No I was not sure. I wanted him to stop yet continue until I blew my load over his hand.

Instead, I placed my hand over his, stopping the motion. My dick screamed *nooooo*.

"Please, stop," I whispered, my breath husky, something it had never been.

Julian actually pouted. "But I don't want to." And he certainly didn't when his hand, underneath mine, continued to stroke me up and down.

"Jesus," I hissed. Closing my eyes, my head fell back. I was embarrassed at how easily he controlled my body.

Julian stepped closer. His heat and his lean, firm body leaned in. I felt his lips at my neck, where he bit. A shudder went through me as my balls shrank up; I was close to coming. "Can I suck your cock, lover-boy?" Julian whispered into my ear, causing me to groan.

No. Yes. No.

Hell yes.

Nodding, Julian made a sound of approval in the back of his throat. Maybe he knew I would chicken out because he quickly pulled the towel apart with one hand, the other stayed around my hardness as he kissed his way down my chest, my stomach and finally, before his mouth surrounded my cock, he looked up at me and smiled.

As soon as his lips parted and glided over my dick, I embarrassed myself by coming like a horny teenager and kept coming as Julian drank it all down.

I collapsed back on my elbows, breathing heavily. Julian grinned down at my flushed cheeks, and then leaned over to kiss my chest, running his tongue around my nipple. My dick jerked.

He wanted more.

Already.

Again and again.

As Julian's mouth caressed me, his hand snuck up and took hold of mine. I supported my weight on one elbow as he guided it down to the front of his slacks. He let go for all but a moment as he undid his pants and pulled his big cock free. There he took hold of my hand again and wrapped it around his arousal. I brushed my fist around his dick and then slid it up and down, ripping a moan from his mouth so it caressed my chest.

"Yes, baby. That feels so good," he uttered.

His words sent a thrill through me. My softened cock jumped

from his words, and my stomach took flight with thousands of butterflies. He liked my hand on him and I wanted to undo this magnificent man. My grip tightened. He groaned and thrust his hips forward, then back.

"Oh, God. Yes, poppet. I'm going to come." And he did. He bit down on my nipple as he ejaculated all over my hand and legs.

After he calmed down, he lifted his head and smiled a sweet, satisfied smile at me. It was then he leaned forward more, as though he was going to kiss me, but it didn't get that far, because I freaked.

Pushing at his chest, he stood and took a step back. I wrapped the towel back around myself and jumped from the table. "I-I need to go," I said without meeting his gaze.

Glancing out the corner of my eyes, I saw him place his cock back in his pants. My own dick was once again hard. He must have noticed it behind the towel because he said, "Are you sure you have to? I could help with that *again*?" I watched his hand gestured to my area that was begging for release.

He took a step toward me. I took one away. "No, that, no, we shouldn't have done that."

His body stiffened. "Mattie, was that your first time with a man?"

My blush would have been answer enough. "I have to go," I uttered and swiftly walked from the room.

I hid out in the locker room until I heard him leave the room and the building. I hid out like a pussy, even though I wanted nothing more than to go back in there and play with what I wanted to be mine and only mine.

Fuck. I was afraid of real life and love.

CHAPTER SIX

MATTIE

*I*f I could describe myself in one word, it would be pathetic. Yes, that was me summed up in so many ways. Another week had gone by and all I could think about was Julian, while I worked, when I was home, even eating, he consumed my mind. However, the biggest reason I was pathetic was because that night, I was supposed to be at football practice. I went to the other four during the past week because I knew Julian wouldn't be there.

Thursday arrived.

The day Julian made an appearance.

So I couldn't attend.

Even though I really wanted to...I couldn't.

There was a risk I would want another *hot* encounter with him in the changing rooms, without a care of who was hanging around.

Sulking, I walked up the drive. I'd pretended I went to football practice so my parents didn't think anything was wrong. They were already looking at me strangely in the past week. I'd lost count of the amount of times they'd asked me what was wrong. Of course, I couldn't say, "Oh, nothing, besides the fact that I have a hard-on constantly from a certain masseur." It wasn't something that'd make a happy night-time story.

Opening the front door, my eyes drifted over the living room, but saw no one was there. "I'm home," I called.

Voices in the kitchen paused and Mum called back, "Dinner's ready, come eat."

"I'll just go dump my stuff and be there in a second."

"Son, you can do that later. Get in here," Dad said. Strange, usually they'd want all my shit out of the way so they wouldn't trip on it.

Leaving it beside the front door, I walked into the kitchen and froze.

My mouth dropped open and I swear I gasped like a little girl seeing a pony for the first time. My heart also picked its pace up so fast it hurt inside my chest.

All of those reactions were because Julian was currently sitting at the dining room table with my parents.

Shit. That could not be good in any way.

"Matthew Alexander, you didn't tell me your 'friend' was joining us for dinner tonight," Mum snapped and yes, she actually air quoted friend with her fingers.

And there was my conundrum. Nothing good could come of it.

Julian hid his smirk and offered, "Well, to be fair, Mrs Alexander, I didn't tell Mattie I was coming tonight."

"Oh, isn't that nice. I always love a surprise. Rich never surprises me anymore. It happens after being together for too long. You make sure to keep that up in your relationship. Mattie can be a bit sour like his father sometimes, but if you treat him right, if you keep the spice in the bedroom, things will work out great."

Holllly shit.

My head dipped back to look at the ceiling; please open the world below my feet and drag me in it.

"Mum." I sighed and looked back to her. "I—"

"Mrs Alexander—"

"Oh, call me Nancy, honey."

"Thank you." Julian smiled. "I was going to say that Mattie and I aren't actually together. I was just worried when he didn't turn up to football practice tonight."

"Kid, I thought you went. You've never missed a practice. What's up with that? You've been out of sorts for some time now. Is this about some special guy?"

"Shit, Dad," I growled.

"Watch your mouth, boy. I can—" He suddenly stopped and studied my panicked expression. He looked to Julian and then back to me. Then he abruptly stood from the table and said, "Nancy, you say I never surprise you, so surprise, we're going out for dinner."

"B-but I have it cooked already."

"Woman, get up, I may even take you to the movies." He took hold of Mum's arm and pulled her from her seat.

"Only if you make-out with me in the movies and buy me popcorn."

"Jesus, woman. Fine." He sighed out the word like it was some huge task. I called bullshit because I was always—insert shudder —witness to their fawning all over each other.

"Bye, boys. Julian, so great to meet you. Hopefully, I'll see you around."

Julian didn't get to reply. Instead, we heard the front door being closed behind them. I faced the living room. Julian, I knew, was sitting calmly on the chair behind me, as my mind freaked out.

"I'm sorry for showing up. It honestly didn't cross my mind you still lived with your parents. You act a lot older than most your age. And once your mum opened the door, there was no escape. She practically dragged me in here."

Snorting, I said, "That doesn't surprise me." Turning to face him, I added, "I'm in the process of getting my own place."

He nodded, more to himself than me as he watched me, and then, shit, his eyes raked over my body, and instantly, I grew hard. To hide it from him, though I doubt I did, I sat in the seat at the end of the table away from the man I fantasised about every night.

"Mattie…"

"Why are you here? How did you find this place? Why are you here? You shouldn't be here, I, this…I'm going insane," I mumbled, my hands going over my face as I shook my head back and forth.

A chair creaked. Julian was up and moving. I tensed when his heat appeared right in front of me. He pried my hands away and I looked up to see him standing before me. He smiled sadly. "I'm sorry if coming here has upset you, meeting your parents…" He grinned and got to his knees in front of me, with my wrists still in his hands. His thumbs circled the back of them, causing my dick to jolt. "Why do they think you're gay, Mattie?"

Shit.

Shaking my head, I mumbled, "I don't know what you're talking about." Lame to deny it, but I was scared.

Scared to let myself *feel* when Julian was around.

All I wanted to do was wrap myself around him and beg him to play.

Beg him to want me and need me, *just me.*

Julian giggled. "I think you do. Handsome, it's okay to…like the same sex. I haven't turned out too bad and I've been doing it for a terribly long time."

My eyes moved from his handsome face to the tiled floor next to us. "Don't, please," I pleaded, only I didn't know what I was pleading for.

"Mattie, poppet." He tugged on my wrists until I was looking at him. I watched as he licked his lips, my own lips mimicked his. He smiled and then asked, "Did you like what we did in that room?"

A pleasant shudder ran throughout my body from just thinking of it.

"I'll take that as a yes." Julian chuckled. He stood and paced the floor in front of me. "I liked it, almost more than I should. I...I came here tonight to let you know, that what you feel, liking men, it's okay to do so. You can't let other bastards get to you. One day, I hope you'll understand that, and learn to be who you want to be, to like whoever you want to like and not worry about what anyone else thinks." He stopped and turned to me. "You'll always get the muff-munchers who hate gay people, no matter where you go. You tend to learn who will be okay and who won't It's those you steer clear of. If they want to get in your face about it, let them have at it...shit, I'm rambling." He laughed. "Anyway, I just wanted to check on you, see if you're okay and let you know you're not the only one to go through this. Any gay guy would be willing to help you through this." He rolled his eyes. "*Any* gay man would shove another over a cliff to be the one to help you...in any way." He winked. I shook my head and lowered it, my mind running with thoughts.

Maybe it was time to man up. Be who I wanted to be. Hell, it was some scary shit to go through. But Julian was right. I wasn't the only one to have been through it.

Goddammit. I'd been a weakling for a long time and never

51

had I considered I wasn't the only one to go through it. Of course there were others.

If others could do it, come out…maybe I could as well.

"Anyhow, I had better go, can't keep my date waiting," Julian chirped. He started for the front.

He had a date?

He'd come here to check on me before his date?

Would he kiss his date?

Would he take that date home?

Fire erupted inside my chest. I didn't like any of those thoughts *at all*.

In seconds, I was out of my chair and striding toward Julian. Grabbing his arm, I turned him and demanded, "Is that supposed to make me jealous?"

Julian actually looked startled. "What? I…no. I'm—"

"You can't do that, Julian. You can't make me crazy. You can't turn me on all the Goddamn time. Come *here* to *this* house to tell me you were worried. You can't look the way you do at me and not have it affect me every time I'm in a room with you." My breathing escalated and then I leaned in, so our noses nearly touched and I growled, "You can't go on a date with anyone, but me." I threaded my hand into the back of his hair and tugged. His mouth touched mine, but it wasn't enough. I demanded entrance. Once he opened up to me, things went a little crazy. We kissed. It was my first real, passionate kiss with a man, and I fucking loved it. My other arm wound around his waist. I dragged him closer. Our bodies touched, our erections rubbed up against each other, and we moaned. His arms wrapped around my waist, a tight grip on my tee as he ground his hard-on against mine.

I pulled back to catch my breath. "Jesus." I tilted my neck as Julian kissed down it.

"No, poppet, just Julian, with one raging boner."

I chuckled. I couldn't help it. I loved the things that came out of his mouth. Hell, I loved his mouth. He slid one hand down my side, over my arse and then dipped around to the front where he caressed my hard cock over my jeans, rubbing it up and down with a firm hand. However, if I let him continue, I'd blow in my boxers and that'd be just awkward. Imagine me explaining to Mum why I was doing the laundry since I'd never done it before. That was not a scene I wanted to take part in.

My hand landed over his to stop his movement. He lifted his head, one brow quirked up in question. "I feel weird doing this."

"Oh," he said and backed off a step.

I reached out, but dropped my hand again. "It's not that I don't...want to. I think, no, I *know* I do. But..." I ran a hand through my hair. "This is my parents' home. I've lived here my whole life. It's weird making out and doing...other things with you in here. In *their* home."

Julian smiled. "I get it. I'd be the same way. How about we trade numbers. I do have to get going."

"On a date?" I growled before thinking.

His smile widened. "You're hotter than chili chips when you're jealous." I glared at him. "It's not a date with a guy. It's with a friend. A *girl* friend. Happy chappie now?"

Rolling my eyes, I nodded. Because knowing that titbit of information, lifted the weight off my chest. I took the phone he offered and passed mine over to him. We added our numbers in and after I passed back his phone, he moved off to the front door once again.

"Do you..." I started and then clammed up.

He looked over his shoulder and asked, "What?"

Heat spread over my face. I had never done this before. Looking to the carpet, I asked, "Do you want to...hang out sometime?"

A giggle filled the room. I looked up in time to see him walk my way. He stopped right in front of me, his hand going to the back of my neck. "I do worry about the age difference—"

"I don't," I spat.

He laughed. "I know, I can tell. But as I was saying, sugar-dick, I do worry about the age difference, but it won't keep me away. Not when a man like you can turn my cock hard in seconds. I'm annoyed to leave here with the deepest shade of blue balls, but I look forward to when we...see each other next. In other words, yes, Mattie, I want to go on a date with you." He leaned in and gently touched his lips to mine. He then whispered against them, "I know you're scared, but I'll be there for you." When he pulled back, I nodded once. He grinned, ran his thumb over my lower lip and said, "You're too good looking, I'm going to have to beat them off with a stick."

I smirked. "Or you could just beat me off?"

He stared for a second and then threw his head back and laughed loudly. As soon as he calmed, he kissed me one last time and said, "I'm out of here before I attack you on your parents' floor." He made it to the door before he said over his shoulder, "And, handsome, I'm privileged you want to take this step with me; I'm horny as hell, but ecstatic you picked me."

"There was no other option for me," I told him. His face softened before he smiled, winked, and left.

CHAPTER SEVEN

JULIAN

*M*y heart was having problems. It felt extra big in my body and I only had one person to blame. Matthew Alexander and his sweet, honey-dipped words. *There was no other option for me.* He shouldn't have said those words because it made me obsessed. My dick was constantly poking at the zipper behind my pants just thinking about all the good, dirty things I could do with the man. I was shocked he hadn't been with another guy, though happy, so very happy that I could break out into song, but shocked he hadn't let another man touch him. He wanted me.

Me!

Little, old, over-the-top-gay me.

Oh, snap a dick in half.

People were looking at me strangely.

Why?

Because I could have squealed from the thought of being Mattie's first...everything.

I didn't understand why he wanted to be my...whatever we were. I didn't want to label us just yet; he was still in the scared process of everything. I knew, from the kiss encounter, that I wanted to be Mattie's boyfriend. What worried me though was the fear in Mattie's eyes. My assumption was that he'd not long ago come out to his parents.

What I wanted would be a big step for him.

Risking losing him wasn't an option. I had never felt so hot for another in all my gay years before. So taking it slow was all I could do, and even if I had to tackle my dick every damn time I saw him, I would do it. *He* wasn't seeing the light of day until Mattie gave it the green go sign.

My phone beeped. I stopped the grocery trolley to pull it out of my back pocket and a smile so wide I was surprised I didn't blind people spread across my face at seeing Mattie's name there. *You have ruined me!*

My brows rose high. I wasn't sure the message was good. *How?*

His answer was fast, thank the gay God. *I can't stop thinking about you. I'm getting no work done. Boss will kill me!!!*

A giggle fell from my mouth. *Awe, poor baby :(I can easily fix that.* I sent that and then quickly held my phone up and snapped a picture of myself smiling. *Now you can look at me instead of thinking of me. You may be able to work then...though, it is doubtful. I am unforgettable. Frank Sinatra even made a song about me.*

His reply was: *Snort! What are you doing tonight?*

My heart skipped a beat. *Now my usual reply would be YOU... but I'm trying my best to be a gentleman. So I will say: Nothing, did you have something in mind?*

I'd like to see your place.

Bang a butthole.

He didn't actually say I could *not* do him.

Oh, God. Matthew Alexander wanted to come to my place. My place where we could be alone. Together. Alone.

Giddiness of pleasure swept through me. My hands shook as I texted him my address and: *I'll even cook you dinner like a good kitchen bitch. 7PM good?*

Great! See you then.

Can't wait. And I couldn't. Heck, it was like I was going on *my* first date. My heart was just about in my mouth with nerves. I couldn't stop smiling from the excitement and I wanted to run down the aisle, jump and click my heels together. Instead, I fought that urge and continued shopping, thinking of the best meal I could make for Mattie.

What was the best meal?

Meat.

Meat on a stick.

Meat in a bun

Meat that was stuffed in...

Sugar on toast, I had to stop thinking of Mattie's meat in all those events or I was going to blow in my pants. Not that I minded, but I hated sticky situations, unless it was in the bedroom.

MATTIE

Looking at Julian's photo for the fiftieth time that day still brought the same effect. My heart would beat double time, my hands would shake and I'd grin like a fool. I couldn't believe I had the balls to text him first, but I did, and even though I was scared, I was happy that I was seeing him.

Dressed in jeans and a white shirt, I climbed the stairs in

Julian's stylish apartment complex. Stopping at door number 4, I knocked and waited with sweaty palms, tingling from head to foot, and my heart beating around in my chest like it was doing the rumba. It picked up its pace once more when I heard footsteps approaching the door.

It swung open and a grinning Julian stood in the open doorway. Our gazes swept over each other. He looked hot in his slacks and navy tee. My eyes went to his face to see him smirking at me. He licked his lips and again, like my own lips were twins with his, I licked mine as well.

"Hey, poppet," he said and then took my hand in his and dragged me to him. Next, his lips were on mine, and with no other thought, I devoured his mouth. One arm wrapped around his waist to force his body tighter to mine, and my other hand wound into his hair to grip it. He groaned.

Damn the man, I couldn't get enough of him. I was ready to yell fuck dinner and take him to his room instead, which shocked the hell out of me.

"Get a room." I heard a female voice behind me say.

Unlatching myself, I looked over my shoulder to see the woman who was with Julian when we had been at the same club. She was grinning at us. Julian shifted and he looked over my shoulder. "Don't be jealous, honey. Just because you can't have this fine specimen of man in your arms."

"That is true, which is why I don't mind the show. Can I come in and watch?"

Saliva slipped down the wrong way when I swallowed hard and then I choked it back up. Julian patted me on the back and I heard laughter coming from his neighbour. Her next comment had my eyes widening. "Julian, you have to teach him to swallow properly so he doesn't choke on it."

"Wench, get out of here before you really scare him." Julian

laughed, pulled me further in and slammed the door to her cack-
ling as she walked down the stairs. "I'm sorry about Melissa.
She's a beast and doesn't know how to act around real human
beings. Though, she is also an awesome neighbour and friend."
He went to step away, taking me with him because my hand was
in his, but stopped when he realised I wasn't moving. He looked
at me and his smile faded a little. "What's wrong?"

Biting my bottom lip, I blushed and focused on the floor.
"She's right. I wouldn't know the first thing about what to do
with you. I could be totally useless in bed. What happens if I do
choke when...shit, I can't even say it."

"Baby," Julian whispered. I could hear the humour in his voice
and I felt even worse. I was fucking useless. I wanted to leave. I
wanted to bolt from the apartment and hide, live out the rest of
my miserable life as a virgin. That was until Julian stepped up to
me. His hands gently went to my cheeks, lifting my face. Our
gazes caught. "It *will* come naturally. You don't need to worry
about it. You'll please me no matter. What happens if I don't
make you happy?"

Snorting, I replied, "I doubt it."

"And I doubt you'll not please me. Take each step as it
comes...and hopefully, we'll both come. But it doesn't have to be
tonight. We don't have to do anything other than enjoy each
other's company while eating dinner."

"I want something to happen," I admitted with another blush.

"Thank snicker doodles for that. I would have jumped your
bones before you made it out the door."

"I-I'm just not sure what—"

He gently touched his lips against mine. "Doesn't matter what
we do as long as we have fun doing it with each other. Whatever
you're not comfortable with tell me and I won't ever cross that
line. I can promise you, Mattie, I won't force you to do anything

you don't like." Once he received a stiff, nervous nod from me, he continued, "Now, let's go and have some dinner. After that, we'll watch a movie and see where the night leads us." He winked and tugged me toward the kitchen.

Dinner was amazing. Julian made a creamy fettuccini pasta, with baked cheesy bread. "Have you always wanted to be a masseur?" I asked after we'd finished eating. It was just one of the many questions that flew around his small two-seater table that night.

"Actually, yes. I enjoy it, talking to new people all the time. I also work part-time in a spa retreat, but I branched out to do home calls as well. Some people are just too embarrassed to enter the resorts because of how they look. They've always wanted a massage, but worry judgment would come with it." He shrugged. "At least in their homes they feel safer."

I nodded my understanding. "How'd you come about being the man for the football team?"

His smile left his face for the first time that night. He looked down at the table as though he was ashamed by the answer. "My father got me the job."

Quietly, I asked, "Is that why you wanted to leave on the first day? Because your dad got the job for you?"

"In a way, yes. My father and I don't see eye to eye. My mother either." I could tell he didn't like the topic of his parents and I hated that for him. I hated whatever they'd put him through and I found myself wishing I'd known him back then to help him with whatever they'd done. Suddenly, he snorted and looked to me. "They're nothing like your amazing parents."

Chuckling, I said, "No, mine are just embarrassing."

Julian laughed. "I have never met anybody like them before. No mother has told me to 'keep the spice in the bedroom.'"

Groaning, I sat back in the chair and warned, "Don't remind me."

"Back on work subjects, I've never asked what you do, when you're not at uni or football."

"I work casually at a real estate agency. I got my certificate last year from online studying. I only do Saturday mornings and Wednesdays."

His head went to the side and I found that cute. "So you did online studying as well as university? What's your major at uni?"

"Business, one day I hope to have my own agency."

He smirked. "You're very focused for a guy your age."

Shrugging, I admitted, "I had nothing else to do. I wasn't one to want to party, pick up girls...I—" A blush rose.

"I understand your need to hide that you're gay, Mattie. I did the same, but with all this fabulousness it's hard to hide what I love, which is men's cocks."

I coughed out a strangled laugh. "You're amazing the way you are, Julian. It's why I liked you from the start."

His eyes widened. "You liked me from the first day?" He sounded as though he thought I was lying.

"I was semi-hard when I saw you and then when you placed your hands on me... Let's just say the table would have been messy if that massage was longer."

His loud laughter filled the kitchen. My chest puffed out because I caused him to laugh like that. I wanted to do it again and again. Just like I wanted to do so many other things to him.

"Wow, ah, maybe talking about being hard isn't best right now," Julian suggested.

True, because my cock was aching and hard behind my jeans.

"Let's go watch the movie," he suddenly announced, standing from the table and quickly turning with his plate to deposit it in the sink.

Was he just as hard as I was?

Standing, I picked up my own plate and took it over to the sink where Julian was rinsing his. I walked up behind him and with all my courage, I lined my body with his. He tensed, only to take a deep shuddering breath and sag against me.

After sitting my plate in the sink, I rested my chin on his shoulder and asked, in a low seductive tone, one I didn't know I had, "Are you hiding something from me, Julian?"

"W-what do you mean?" he asked as he picked up my plate and started rinsing it. He jumped slightly when I placed my hands on his slim, yet firm hips.

"I think you know what I mean."

"Nope," he said, shaking his head.

"No? Well, let's see then." My heart beat hard in my chest. I was a nervous wreck. Yet still, slowly, I ran one hand down his side, around to his front and over his erection that was hidden behind his pants. He gasped.

"Don't worry, I found what you're hiding." I smiled when he groaned, dropping the plate in the sink so he could brace his hands on the edge as I ran a tight hand up and down his hardness.

Ecstatic. That was how I felt because I was the one who had started it. However, the jumble of nerves settled deep in my belly had me worried that I would somehow stuff up this seduction and look like a fool.

Yet something also told me that even if I did, Julian wouldn't judge me or care.

"You're a man of many hidden talents, poppet. I didn't know super sight was one of them," Julian teased and pushed his cock more into my hand.

"It was a good guess, babe, since I was sporting one as well. You seem to have that effect on me."

"Oh, God, if you keep going, I'll come," he warned.

"We can't have that...yet." Moving my hand, I placed it back on his hips and turned him quickly to face me. Positioned before me, I slanted my lips down on his and wrapped my arms around his waist more so I could take that extra step where our bodies lined. I rubbed my own erection against his cock and wondered if his was throbbing as much as mine. As my groans were silenced by his lips, Julian slapped his hands onto my arse and pulled me tighter to him.

"Jesus," I panted, placing my forehead onto his shoulder. It was easy because he was that little bit taller than me. "We, um, should watch that movie," I suggested, because if we didn't stop, I was sure things would soon be out of control.

"Mattie, poppet. I... fuck, I can't stop now. I need you."

Lifting my head, I stared into his heated gaze. "How?"

"Precious, I want you to fuck me. I need to have you fill me with your cock and fuck me hard, so I can still feel you tomorrow."

"Fuck," I whispered. "I-I want this to be good for you too."

Julian giggled. "It'll be great for me." He pecked my lips. "Bedroom?" Biting my bottom lip, I nodded. "Aw, it's so cute you've gone all shy now when only moments ago you were the one driving me crazy."

Laughing, heat rose to my cheeks. "That was pretty much all the courage I had."

He leaned forward and kissed my neck. "I'm glad for it. I'm super-duper happy to know you want me as much as I want you." After straightening, he took my hand from his waist and stepped toward the bedroom. The hallway wasn't long so I was grateful we were in his bedroom in seconds. If it had of been longer, I would have run screaming because my sudden anxiety was overwhelming. However, once I was through his bedroom door and Julian took his shirt off, I was too surprised to think anything other than the fact that I was *really* about to have sex with a man. A sexy, buff man.

Licking my lips, Julian teasingly undid the top button to his slacks and unzipped them. "I think I'm getting ahead of myself.

You need to catch up." He smiled, and that smile had me gripping the bottom of my shirt and pulling it up over my head. I undid my jeans and pushed them down, jumping around while I removed my shoes and socks. I stood back up to see an amused Julian.

CHAPTER EIGHT

JULIAN

*H*e was amazing, absolutely mouth-watering amazing. A tiny bit shorter than myself, but at the perfect height. His frame was larger than mine, but only slightly. I appreciated every defined muscle from the hard workouts he did for football, eager for a touch.

In fact, I was prepared to get to my knees and worship the ground he walked on.

No, bugger that thought. Instead, I would worship every bump and dip on the man's body.

And he was a man, no other his age had the maturity that he did. And no other man had the edible package that was currently forming a tent in his black boxers.

My heart, head, and soul were fit to burst with the raging emotions swirling through me.

Matthew Alexander was in my room wanting *me* to be his

first, waiting for me to fulfil his needs. And it was exactly what I would do.

Anything my poppet wanted I would do and that thought was scary. He could crush me in moments, but I was willing to take a risk on him. There was no logic to it. It simply *was*. I had no other choice. Like Mattie *had* said, there was no other choice. He was it for me and there would be, in no way, shape, or form, I would miss what was about to happen.

"Do you need some help?" Mattie asked.

Snorting, more to myself than anyone, because I did indeed need help since my emotions were overriding me, like a wild fire inside of me. I was also worried that I'd move too fast for him. There was a chance that as soon as I had my hands on his silky skin, I'd be even crazier with need, with the need to claim him for myself and no one else.

Giving him a playful wink I said, "I could use some help."

He smiled and stalked over to me as his eyes raked over my naked chest with desire. My cock bobbed behind my slacks. *He* wanted Mattie's eyes on him, wanted Mattie preening all over him, telling him how wonderful *he* was. Okay, I was going overboard, but I swear my cock had a mind of its own because when Mattie was in front of me, gripping my pants and slowly sliding them down until my dick sprang free—I wasn't one to wear underwear—I swear on my hidden gay porn that it waved at Mattie.

All thoughts left my brain and my heart flatlined when Mattie growled, "I want to suck your cock."

"Mmhfphe," was my reply. Mattie chuckled. He liked that he was undoing me. Something that had never been possible before with my precious lovers.

Amusement left his features and was replaced with lust. His eyes darkened as he stepped closer, his hand winding around my cock. He kissed my neck and I arched as I moaned my pleasure. His lips trailed to my ear, where he whispered in a deeper voice than usual, "Do you want my lips around your cock, Julian?"

If I didn't feel his rapid heart beating against my own chest or the way his hands lightly shook, I would have thought Mattie had done seduction a million times. At the end of the night, I was certainly grading him an A+++ for the way he drove me wild.

"Yes," I whispered back and was rewarded with his lips smiling against my neck. Leisurely, he trailed his mouth along my body, kissing the whole way down. If my dick could talk, it would have said, "Stop with the torture already and hurry the fuck up. Kiss me. Love me, make me come." However, *I* was enjoying the time he took, as though he was cherishing every inch of me.

When he was on his knees, he palmed my dick, rubbing it up and down as he looked up at me, his cheeks a deep shade of red. I wasn't sure if he was asking me with his eyes if it was okay, if I was enjoying it, but all I could do was nod and smile.

He kissed the tip of it and if Mattie hadn't been holding my dick already, it would have jumped in joy. A lick around the tip was next, a moan from both of us. He'd enjoyed tasting my pre-cum, something that made me happy. In the next second, one hand dropped to the back of my bare thigh, while his other hand, and soon his head, was bobbing up and down. His hot mouth surrounded my erection, and like a pro, he sucked, licked and tongued all over me.

"Poppet, fuck, that feels good, so good," I uttered. His hands disappeared and I wondered where they'd gone. In the next moment, he cupped my balls, gently massaging them. His other hand went into the front of his boxers. He started to stroke himself, until I ordered, "Stop touching yourself. Leave that for me."

His mouth left my cock. He groaned painfully and then

growled, "I need to come. Shit, I never thought giving head would turn me on so much. I'm about to blow."

Stepping back, I said, "Lie down on the bed, poppet. I'll help you with that."

He stood. "But...I liked what I was doing. Didn't you?" He blushed. My man could be so deliciously shy. He was an enigma, hovering between dominant and innocence and I loved every blush as much as every order.

"Never doubt yourself with me, Mattie. I loved it. If I could have your mouth around my cock twenty-four-seven, I would. Though, it'd be a bit awkward explaining it while walking down the street." I chuckled and then took matters into my own hands. I slipped my feet out of my slacks, walked over to the bed, and lay flat in the middle. Up on my elbows, I watched as Mattie's eyes perused my body with a wicked gleam. His chest rose and fell in swift movements. "Now, lover-boy, you may continue as you were, but I want to suck your cock at the same time." His body stilled, until he smiled, discarded his boxers and bounced his way to me on the bed. Before he turned his glorious body around, he leaned over me and kissed the daylights out of me, leaving me panting, breathless, nearly seeing stars, and it was only the start.

The man was going to ruin me in good, delicious ways.

Without words, Mattie, with a deep blush coating his cheeks, got to his hands and knees, shifting around. He placed his knees on each side of my head and then his hands dipped the bed at my hips, on each side. Reaching between his legs, I took hold of his erection and pointed it back toward me. A desire-filled grunt left his lips as I lifted my head and sucked his cock deep into my eager mouth. His body shuddered over me.

"Christ, Julian, that feels good," he growled before bracing on one hand as his other wrapped around my hardness and aimed it up to his mouth. He twirled his tongue around it and then slid his wet lips down, touching the base. I moaned around him in my mouth. He gagged once, and then retreated.

How could a man who had never given head before be so good? It was beautifully unnatural. Consumed with happiness and desire knowing I found the gem before anyone else, I expected to be afraid when the thought of keeping him to myself for the rest of my living life crossed my mind. I wasn't.

God, I was going to come soon if he kept his good work up. I needed to change it up a little, take the control back. I let his dick fall from my mouth with a pop. From there, I grabbed his arse and brought it down closer to my mouth. He stilled as I angled my neck, my own cock falling from his mouth when I took the first lick over his puckered hole.

"Julian, I-um, I don't think…"

"Then don't think. Feel." I went back to licking and kissing around, up and down and on his hole.

"Jesus," he growled, arching his back a little, giving me more access to himself. I knew what he was thinking. We all went through it—that we shouldn't like what was happening, that it was wrong to like it. But what he was feeling overrode any thoughts.

Placing my head back on the bed, I watched his body for signs of regret, of anything that would tell me I needed to stop. I took my hand from his hip, spat on a finger and traced it around his puckered ring. Rubbing it over and over it until he pushed back on my finger a little, which was how I knew he wanted more. Gently, I pushed my finger slowly inside of him.

"Julian," he groaned.

"It's okay," I whispered. Further in, his body tensed. It was an uncomfortable feeling to start with, but once I was all in and playing, he would be begging for more. "Just relax, poppet," I said. Moving my other hand, I wound it around his throbbing cock and jacked him off, easing some of the discomfort. He took a deep breath and when he did, I thrust my whole finger in.

"Fuck," he cried when I hit his prostate. "God, ah fuck, Julian," he moaned as I rubbed my finger up and down inside of him.

"Feel good, baby?"

"Yes," he breathed. "Yes." He then dove for my cock, his wet mouth pumped up and down on it. The motion helped him rock back and forth on my finger. He moaned and hummed around me. Watching him enjoy his first fingering had my balls shrinking up quickly. I let go of his cock, knowing he'd be able to blow his load just from arse action.

"Oh, God, poppet, suck me, yes, like that." I groaned.

His arse was eager now, hitting back hard on my finger. He slid his mouth to the tip of my cock and then his mouth was gone from me as he cried out, "I'm gonna come." Mattie sucked my pulsating cock back into his mouth.

He stilled for all but a second and then fucked my finger hard as I felt his cum shoot out all over my stomach. As soon as the first touch hit me, my own load shot forward into Mattie's mouth. He grunted as he kept coming while swallowing mine down.

"God, yes, take it, take all of me," I moaned and he did. He drank it all down like a master.

As soon as he collapsed on me, his head hitting my hip, I gently and slowly removed my finger; he twitched from it. I knew he would be blushing like Snow White's lipstick; the first time was always the most awkward.

He rolled to his side. I sat up and looked down at him, his breathing rapid, his arm thrown over his eyes and, as I thought, his cheeks were red.

"I find it hard to believe that was your first time," I said.

"Why?" he asked, only he wouldn't remove his arm so I could see his beautiful green eyes.

"That was the best head anyone has given me."

He snorted. "Yeah, sure."

Frustrated he was still hiding, I moved around until I was lying next to him. I kissed his chest and pried his arm away and then held his hand. He turned his head to look at me. I smiled. "Once you get to know me, you'll find that I don't lie...or else my penis grows which could be good, but...I'm kidding. Still, ask Melissa, I don't lie and I hate anyone who lies to me. Matthew Alexander, your mouth on my cock, the way you sucked it, licked it and did all those wicked things to it was the best I have ever had. And for that reason alone, you can't blame me..."

He smirked. "For what?"

"Kidnapping you. You're all mine now," I uttered, my tone serious and then I bit his shoulder.

He chuckled. "That sounds okay to me."

I lifted my head. "Really?"

"Well, yeah. I wouldn't have...wanted to do any of this with you if I didn't want you as my..." He blushed.

"You can say it, come on," I teased.

He rolled his eyes. "Boyfriend."

"Good boy." I giggled. There was something I needed to know, so I rested on my elbow and looked down at my man. "Did...did you like what I did?"

He closed his eyes, his cheeks heating once again. "Yes. I'm sure you could tell."

"Have you ever played down there yourself?"

He peeked out at me and shook his head.

Smiling, I said, "If I had feathers right now, they would be puffed out like the proudest peacock in the world. I like that I'm the first to touch your arse, Mattie. I like it very much." To state how much, I shifted my hip into his side so he'd feel my growing erection.

He burst out laughing, wrapped his arm around my shoulders

71

and dragged me on top of him. "You're too cute, Julian." He smiled and jutted his hips up, causing our cocks to rub together and I felt him grow instantly. "Can we...play again?"

Shaking my head, I said, "No."

"No?" he mimicked.

"No, this isn't play time. This is serious business, Matthew Alexander, because I want you to fuck me." He moaned, wrapped both arms around me and pulled my head down where his lips and tongue mingled nicely with mine. "I need your cock inside me, poppet."

"Fuck yes," he growled. "Get on your knees," he ordered. Panting, because hell, that man just turned it up a notch to hotter than Chris Hemsworth when he spoke all in charge like that. I repositioned myself to my hands and knees beside him. He stayed lying next to me, just looking up with a heated gaze, eyes roaming my naked body. Even though I was taller than him, he made me feel small; he made me feel desired and wanted.

"Lube?" Mattie asked.

For the first time that night, I blushed. The fine specimen of man shifted to his knees and wanted to join with me. Knowing it was his first time, I was nervous for him and myself. If he didn't like it, I wouldn't know what the hell to do. Even though what we'd already shared proved there was hope I'd blow his mind not only his load, I still worried.

"Top drawer." I couldn't help but giggle when Mattie, with the speed of Flash, got from the bed, pulled the drawer open, and threw the tube of lube onto the bed.

"Are you sure you want me to do this?" Mattie asked quietly as he climbed up behind me.

"If you don't, you'll soon find me tackling you and having my wicked way anyway."

"What about a condom?" Mattie asked. Usually, I would be all over it and have one ready on the bed...but I didn't want anything between the two of us. I'd never wanted that before in my life.

Looking over my shoulder to him, I said on a shrug, "I'm clean."

He nodded, smiled and said, "So am I."

Then I blurted, "I've never gone unprotected before, never." Staring at him, I hoped he understood what I meant. The way his eyes softened and warmed told me he did.

Mattie chuckled nervously and then he sobered, his face serious. "Shit, I-I don't know how to act. My mind is telling me to be dominant, take control, but my heart is telling me to be... nervous and scared and worried. I don't want to stuff this up, Julian. I want you to want me to come back again and again."

Turning, I sat down on the bed and looked up at him on his knees before me, his hard cock pointing out, his firm body beaded with sweat. I placed my hands on his thighs and ran them over his body as I said, "Right now, I like how your mind is thinking. I'd love for you to take control. Tell *me* what to do and if I don't, punish me." He groaned. "Then again, I also understand everything else you're feeling, but I can assure you everything takes practice and I'll love everything you do, no matter how you do it. Christ on crack, I've already enjoyed myself immensely. So much so, I'm worried I'll turn stalker on your cute arse." I kissed his stomach as he laughed. Funny thing, I wasn't sure I was joking about that part. Resting my chin on his stomach and getting poked in the neck by a certain impatient part of him, I looked up and met his gaze. "For now, go with your mind and body. They both know what they want, what you want."

He gave me a stiff nod. His jaw clenched and I wondered if he was trying to hold back from attacking me. I was about ready to tell him to go for it when he hissed, "Get to your fucking knees, Julian."

A shudder rushed through me and then I did as I was told,

hiding my smile while doing it. Once situated in front of him, his hands went to my shoulders and he roughly pulled my arse back so it collided with his hips. There he rubbed his erection up and down and his hands ran down my back. One hand glided around to cup and play with my balls while the other slapped me on the arse. A cry of pleasure came from my mouth, my head snapped up.

"You liked that, Julian?" Mattie demanded and slapped my arse again. I gripped the sheets under my hands and nodded. "I can't hear you, Julian." Another smack, this one harder. I was sure he felt my balls drawing up into my body. If he kept the assault up on me, I was going to come, without even penetration. "Julian," he growled, gripped my hair and pulled my head back and to the side so he could see my face. What he saw had him smiling with satisfaction. He knew he was driving my body crazy. "Pass me the lube," he ordered. "I need to fuck you before you come."

"Yes," I moaned. My body was humming with anticipation. Quickly passing back the tube, I felt his hands leave my body, heard the tube being popped open and the squirt of lube coating his fingers. Looking over my shoulder, I watched his hand cover his dick and slick lube all over it. He knew I was watching and he put on a show for me, gliding his hand up and down, again and again. I loved how he handled himself. While I watched, his other hand caused me to jump slightly when I felt it on my arse. Then his fingers slid between my cheeks and ran the sticky substance over my puckered hole.

"God, Mattie," I uttered and pushed back on his fingers.

"Keep still," he hissed and the bed dipped as his knees edged closer to my arse. His fingers left the tight ring, and with one hand on my hip and the other hand guiding him in, the tip of his cock slowly breached my passage. "Fuckin' hell, you're tight."

"Hmmmm," I moaned and moved my arse back so he slipped in a little more before he slapped my arse again.

"Don't move," he growled.

"Please, Mattie, please."

"Fuck, just a minute," he hissed. I wasn't sure if it was meant for me or himself. His hands clamped down on my hips harder. I felt the first drop of his sweat on my back. He was holding himself back so he didn't hurt me. Oh, God. He was precious. "I can't...I have to..." He needed to get passed the resistance inside of me and then we'd both feel great. Though, I was sure he was already feeling it, I just needed more of him in me. Thankfully, I didn't have to wait long. One hand went to my shoulder and he leaned over my body more, his breath heavy at my neck where he kissed me as he pushed all the way in, both of us groaning from the sensation.

He panted, "You good?"

"God, more than good."

"I need to...Christ." He moaned and started his onslaught of pumping in and out of me, his chest left my back, both hands to my hips as he thrust his cock faster into my arse. "You feel so good."

"Yes, Mattie, God, you feel...yes, right there. Oh, God." I found myself slamming back onto his dick. He moaned and slapped my arse and that was all it took, my balls tucked up into my body and I came all over my bed. "I'm coming, yes, baby, yes, fuck me."

"Jesus," Mattie yelled and I knew why, my arse had just clamped down around his cock as I came for the second time that night. "Fuck, so tight," he screamed. His cock swelled inside of me and then his cum shot out, filling me. "Hell," he panted, resting his sweaty chest on my back, his forehead hitting my shoulder as he slowed his thrusts, coming down from ejaculating so hard. "That was...hell, I want to do it again."

Bursts of laughter filled me and left my mouth. Exhausted, I said, "Baby, we can, but much later. Right now you have to get off me before I crash to the bed and we get injured."

He chuckled, lifting himself off me. When his slack cock pulled slowly from my arse, a shudder raked my body. As soon as he lifted, he was down again and taking me with him. He flopped to the bed, his arm wrapping around my waist dragging me down to his side.

"I forgot you're seventeen years older than me. Of course you need a rest, old man."

Gasping, I straddled his waist and slapped his chest a few times. "You big, mean jock. You're lucky you were the best I've had yet or else I would be kicking your arse out."

"The best?" He smirked. Reaching up with his hand, he placed it at the back of my neck and pulled me down. Before we fell asleep, he kissed and teased me. "You were fucking amazing, Julian. Now get some rest so we can...get serious again."

CHAPTER NINE

MATTIE

a week and a half passed and I could honestly say every moment was amazing. I saw Julian nearly every night and stayed at his house. My parents knew where I was because my mum just happened to ring the morning after our first night together. Julian, barely awake, leaned over to the floor where my phone had fallen from my jeans, and answered it with, "Chello?"

"Mattie?"

I was still half asleep, but when I heard Julian gasp and say, "Oh, shit." I sat up quickly and he practically threw my phone at me saying over and over, "I'm sorry. I'm sorry. I thought it was my phone."

Wondering what was going on, I placed the phone to my ear. "Hello?"

Then I heard a sniffle. "Was that the lovely man, Julian?"

Fuck. "Um, Mum—"

"Was it?" she cried.

Sighing, I answered, "Yes."

"Tell him he's to come to dinner on Wednesday. I need to know more about my son's boyfriend."

In the background, I heard yelling. "Jesus, woman, if our son is at a booty call, then what the hell are you doing on the phone with him? Hang up, Nancy."

"Matthew Alexander. Wednesday, dinner, make sure your boyfriend comes."

"Nancy," Dad yelled.

"Matt?" Mum snapped.

Groaning in pain instead of pleasure, like I wished I was, I said, "Yes, Mum. I'll make sure to tell him."

"Great, bye-bye and don't forget protection." With that, she hung up. I flopped back on the bed closing my eyes and wished it were all just a nightmare.

"Soooo, I, as in, your *boyfriend*, am invited to dinner Wednesday?"

"That really wasn't a nightmare?"

"No, poppet." He giggled and rested on my chest, his chin between my ribs digging in, but I liked it. I opened my eyes and looked down at my...boyfriend and smiled.

"You don't mind, do you?" I asked.

"What? That your parents want to see me again or that your mum called me your boyfriend?"

"Both. You still have time to back out and run like hell," I offered.

His smile was beautiful. "No way, baby. You're stuck with me now."

"Good." I smiled and rolled him to his back where I took advantage of him being under me.

Julian agreed that we keep our relationship a secret, at least for the time being. I hated that I had the urge to hide it still, but I wanted to enjoy and learn about him more before everything blew up in my face. My parents accepted him. Mum loved him, especially when he was willing to help her in the kitchen when we had dinner on the Wednesday. When I arrived home from work, he was already in there talking like they'd known each other for years. Dad thought he was strange, but then said he'd fit into the family better being that way.

In between canoodling during the week, we actually went out on dates...in public. Only, it was to places I knew I wouldn't run into anyone I knew. We went to dinner and the movies and that was when I discovered Julian Jacob's was the biggest flirt in town. No matter who it was, he would say whatever popped into his mind.

It didn't bother me that he said what he wanted. I liked his quirky ways, but what did bother me, what I hated, was when he got a lot of attention from it. Some attention made me posses- sive and jealous. Other attention made me feel on edge and nervous, wondering if he'd get into trouble when he'd say it to the wrong type of person. Thankfully, so far that hadn't happened. They'd either flirt back, which annoyed me, or ignore him, some even laughed at his antics.

Unfortunately, after the second night out and being witness to it—okay, it was mainly because another guy wanted Julian in his bed that night and I didn't like that thought—when we got back to Julian's apartment, we got into a fight. He screamed it was just who he was and he meant nothing by it. He defended that he knew when to stop before it came to fists in his face and he also knew when to stop with the flirting, which was harmless on his part apparently. He did it because he liked to get a reac- tion and that was all. He never wanted any of the men, even if they were gay. He never wanted them because he had me.

I found that hard to believe so I stormed out. That was when I saw Melissa standing in the hallway. She had obviously been listening in. "Come have a chat with Aunt Melissa so she can tell you a story." I wanted to tell her to get fucked, but I also wanted to understand Julian better. I needed to understand him because I was worried for him, for us. I'd come to care for him a great deal, even though we'd only known each other for nearly a month. Melissa knew Julian a lot more than I did, so I walked into her apartment and was glad I did. I learned Julian was the most loyal person she knew and he'd had a very hard, strict upbringing. Most of his life he was controlled by his parents and he was never allowed to be himself. Which was why Julian went above and beyond trying to prove to himself that they hadn't restrained the "real Julian" at all. Then Melissa proceeded to ask me if I was willing to put up with it all and accept and embrace Julian as he was.

Of course I did. I wanted to. The thought of not seeing him was the pits. Nodding to Melissa, I said, "Julian is...a ray of sunshine on a dreary day." I blushed because that had sounded so corny, but it was true. "He *is* an amazing person and my life would be grey without him in it."

When I told her that, she smiled. Tears formed in her eyes and she said, "I'm glad you feel that way about him. He deserves so much in life."

Leaving Melissa's, I planned to let Julian have some time to cool down, but I also didn't want to leave the night as I had— walking out on him. I didn't want him to think I didn't care for him as he was. The flirting may take time to get over, but once I really thought about it, I noticed certain things. While he flirted, he sought out my eyes, or he'd run a hand over me, touching me in some way. If I wasn't next to him, he'd wink at me and smile. Letting me know, in his own way, that he didn't mean anything by it; he was only having fun.

I meant more to him than a quick thrill.

After one knock, his apartment door flew open. His eyes were red, tear stains still evident on his cheeks. "I'm sorry," I said.

I waited for the door to slam in my face. It didn't. Instead, he reached out, pulled me through and slammed the door behind me, then he pushed me against the door, his body fitting as close to mine as he could get.

He sniffed. It was cute. "No, poppet. I'm sorry, so sorry for what I put you through. I'll try to change. I promise. I know I'm not good enough for you..." His breath caught, cracking my heart.

"Don't," I growled and wrapped my arms around him. He placed his head on my chest, his body shaking. "Be who you are, Julian. I like you just as you are. It was my own stupid jealousy I was dealing with. I just worried you were losing interest in me."

"Never." He sniffed again. "That can never happen. I'm your number one stalker now and I'm not letting you go."

That night was different. I stayed and we doted on each other in different ways. We were slow and sensual. It was beautiful. It was us.

It was Thursday and the usual day Julian would be at football practice. He hadn't made it the previous week because he had prior arrangements to see his aunt. When I met him later that night, he seemed upset about something, but he wouldn't tell me. That shadow stayed with him for the rest of the week. Still, he wouldn't confide in me, all he said was that it was family business. I didn't push it, even though I wanted to. I just hoped he'd come to me in the end so I could help.

As I showered the sweat from my body, I found myself nervous as excitement raced through me in expectation. Part of me wondered if my teammates noticed the difference in me. Though, I doubted it; they were wrapped up in their own world. However, I couldn't help but think they could see the small smile on my face just thinking of being in the room with Julian while he rubbed down my body...if we got that far.

Shit, I shouldn't even be thinking of doing anything with him while we were in the changing rooms, but I couldn't help it. I loved having his hands on me and mine on him. Thinking of it caused my cock to harden. Quickly shutting off the water, I roughly wiped myself down and wrapped the towel around my waist. Walking out to the locker room, I noticed only a few players were still hanging around. Seeing Lions walk from the room I knew my boyfriend was in, looking relaxed and happy, pissed me off. Seriously, I had to dampen down my jealousy and it was hard to refrain from walking over to him to knock that look off his face.

"Hey, Alexander. You're up," he said and went to his locker. "Man, if that guy wasn't a dude, I'd marry him. His hands are amazing." He chuckled. I slammed my locker door closed and turned to glare at him. He looked at me with humour in his eyes. "I knew it."

"What?" I snapped and looked around to see we were now alone.

"You have a thing for him." He turned to face me.

"What? I..." *Man up, Alexander.* "Yes."

Lions shrugged. "Don't bother me, bro. To each their own and all that. Just watch some of the others."

Nodding, I said, "I'm not...I don't want them to know yet."

"Hey, I won't say anything."

Sighing, I sent him a chin lift. "Thanks."

"You gonna stay in football when you do come out?"

Shaking my head, I answered, "No, never wanted to play in the first place."

"Good place to hide though." He chuckled. "You're a good player, be sorry to see you leave the team."

"Jesus Christ, Alexander," Coach yelled from outside his

office. "Stop bloody gossiping and get your arse in there so I can get the fuck outta here." He spun around and slammed his door, only to re-open it and throw something at me. I caught the keys just in time. "Forget it," Coach barked. "I'm leavin'. You're locking up. Got a hot date tonight, kid. I ain't missing it." With that, he stalked off out of the change rooms.

Lions and I exchanged amused looks before we burst out laughing. I walked toward the door that held my boyfriend behind it and said over my shoulder, "See you, Lions."

"Yeah, catch ya."

At the door, I knocked once and when I heard Julian say come in, I opened it to see his smiling face. However, he looked like he'd been crying or hadn't slept. Dark circles surrounded his gorgeous eyes and he hadn't shaved either that morning, which was something he hated going without.

"Hey, poppet. You look mighty fine, good enough to eat." He licked his lips. "I heard the coach yelling. We're here alone, right?"

"Yes," I said and walked to the table. "Babe?"

"Hmm?" he replied as he readied his hands with oils.

"You look tired." I lifted myself up to sit on the edge of the table facing him. When he turned around and saw me, his eyes widened. What surprised him, I think, was the serious look upon my face.

"I didn't get much sleep last night, poppet, that's all." His hands went down to his sides, they looked shiny from the oils that coated them, but they were also shaking slightly.

"Julian," I started only to pause and bite my lip. I didn't want to push, but seeing him like that, the worst I had ever seen him, made me worry more so. If he wouldn't talk to me, all I could do was help him forget whatever was plaguing him for the moment. "Come here," I ordered.

He sagged in relief for me not pushing him into talking about whatever was on his mind, and stepped forward into my opened legs. I ran my hands over his black teed chest, only to slip my hands low again and sweep the tee from his body.

My dick pulsated at seeing his smooth skin. He saw it, his hands starting to trail up my thighs, but I stopped them, laying my hands over his. He looked up at me in question. I cupped his cheek. "You're an amazing man, Julian Jacob, and I want you to be my first in every way."

His eyes widened. "W-what do you mean?"

I smirked. "Fuck me."

His head rocked back, shock written all over him. His body tensed, his hands clenched into fists at his sides. "What? Here? Now?" He licked his lips. "As in, you want my meat package to join with your bun package?"

Chuckling, I said, "Yes."

"Here?"

"Yes, I'd like it to be here. We've had a lot of firsts here. When we first met, when we first touched, and now when you first fuck me."

"Poppet, if you keep *telling me* to fuck you, I won't get the chance. I'll come in my pants."

"Well, you better get to it then." I slipped down to stand in front of him. He hadn't made a move to touch me yet, so I helped him undo his pants and pulled them down his legs. I shook my hips and the towel dropped to the floor at our feet. He was breathing heavily, matching my own pants.

God, I wanted Julian in every way I could get him.

I was addicted.

Wrapping my hand around his hard cock, I kissed him. From there on, he took over. He knocked my hand away from his dick as his other gripped my hair at the back of my head. "No, or I'll come. Hell," he breathed. "You are so handsome and *mine*." I loved the possessive tone in his voice. He kissed me hard and rubbed our dicks together before turning me and forcing my chest to the table. "Are you sure about this?"

"God, yes," I said and then moaned when his fingers traced my ring.

Panting, I looked over my shoulder and watched him move around for more oil, coating his other hand in it. He then brought it to my arse, stroking the slippery substance over his fingers and my ring, while his other hand rubbed it over his shaft.

"Julian, fuck me," I hissed. I couldn't wait any longer. I wanted him inside me.

"Shut up, poppet. I'm serious when I said I'd come."

I laughed, only to stop and moan when two of his fingers slipped inside of me, past the resistance. We'd been playing a lot during the week, and the arse play he did on me was driving me wild, so wild I was more than ready for him.

Rocking back on his fingers, I palmed my own cock and started to tug. Then his fingers disappeared and in place, I felt his knob slip and slide over my ring. "Yes," I hissed.

Julian grunted and rested one hand on the table beside my hip. His other hand was around his dick as he applied pressure against my puckered hole. I pushed back against it. "Take it slow," Julian advised.

However, I didn't want to. I pushed again.

"Goddamn, poppet, you're driving me crazy." He nudged more inside of me and then the pain took my breath away. "Breathe, honey, breathe through it and relax." I did. I slowed my breath and made myself clam down. Julian entered a bit further. It still hurt but not as much as before, and then, he was all the way in. His balls slapped into mine and he stayed still, letting me adjust around him.

He leaned forward, his chest touching my back and then

whispered into my ear, "You feel so good, poppet, so bloody good. Your arse is heaven."

Snorting a laugh out, I smiled. When he moved out of me and back in, hitting my sweet spot, I groaned out, "Again." He did and it felt fucking unreal. My hand sped up on my dick. I was just about ready to blow my load all over the floor.

Julian kissed my back and ran his hands all over me as he fucked my arse. "I love your arse. Damn, Mattie, God, you feel so good surrounding me," he panted. "Hell, I'm going to marry your arse." He groaned deeply.

At that point in time, I would just about let him do anything to my arse. Nuptials and all.

"Babe," I hissed. "Fuck, you better come soon."

"So close, poppet, so close."

"I-I'm about to…" I threw my head back and grunted through the jets of sperm shooting from my cock. I'd never come that hard. My vision blinked out for seconds.

"Yes, God, yes," Julian chanted as he fucked me hard and then he swore, growling out through his own release. Julian collapsed onto my sweaty back. "Never had better," he whispered.

Smiling, I tried to lift my head but I couldn't; my body was spent. "And you never will again. You're mine, Julian Jacob."

"Gladly."

CHAPTER TEN

ONE WEEK LATER

JULIAN

*M*y whole life could crumble to a dirty heap at any moment. Relieved I'd spoken to my aunt, who believed me, she was making her move to leave her husband. It hurt seeing the pain in her eyes, the disgust. I hated I was the one to ruin her marriage, even if she thanked me and told me she hadn't been happy for a long time. As soon as my father cottoned on to what I had done, my life was going to be... God, it was going to be agony.

Knowing that was what kept me up at night; I was the cause of my aunt's anguish, all because of my father wanting to rule my life, was what had me hardly eating.

The only thing keeping me going was Mattie.

So even through my torment, I found myself smiling as I lay on my couch while I thought of my man. Mattie had given himself over to me. No other man had. The men before him only wanted to fuck me. I wasn't allowed near their arse.

But Mattie had me.

Mattie wanted me.

He couldn't get enough of me.

Snot a block, he was awesome.

The way it felt, the way Mattie surrendered to me, I couldn't describe it. My heart expanded so much because I felt *so much* that it hurt, but it hurt so good.

I knew I had to talk to Mattie, to let him know everything that was going on in my life, what my parents were like and how much trouble I was about to be in.

I was scared though. Scared he'd see me as weak because I hadn't stood up to my father. Scared that, over my father, I could possibly lose the love of my life.

There wasn't a doubt that it was love. Loving Matthew Alexander was easy.

He made me want so many things. He made me want to be a better person, be in a committed relationship. Again, that was something I had never wanted. He made me feel strong, desired, liked and loved.

My phone chimed beside me on the coffee table. I picked it up and read the message from my poppet, letting me know he would be more than happy to see me that night. Earlier, I'd asked him around for dinner, so I could tell him everything. I refused to believe what I had to say would drive him away. Mattie wasn't like that...but believing it one hundred percent was impossible, because so many people in my life had let me down.

There was a bang at the door, someone using their fist against it. I had a feeling I knew who it was, which was why I didn't go to open the door. Instead, I stayed lying on the couch, covering my ears.

Unfortunately, in the next second, my door was thrown open. I jumped from the couch, my heart taking off in panic. My father stood in the doorway.

"Did you forget I had a key, son?" He smirked. The look in his eyes was feral. I backed up a step, my calves hitting the couch. "You stupid, meddling son-of-a-bitch. How dare you seek your aunt out and tell her things to make her leave my brother." He stepped into my apartment and shut the door with a bang, just like my heart banged to my feet.

Whatever was about to happen wasn't going to be good.

I had to do something myself.

Diving for my phone, which had fallen to the floor, I snapped it up, only it was knocked out of my hand right after. A fist connected with my jaw, knocking me back a step. My father came for me again. I retreated until I was backed up against the wall.

"You've been nothing but a nuisance to me since you were born. Your mother should have had an abortion," he barked in my face.

Not my best move, but I snorted in his face. "I wished she had, then I wouldn't have been born to such a bitch and bastard."

Daddy dearest slapped me across the face for the comment. "I'll make you regret going to her and then I will hunt them down and make her regret it by delivering your stupid little cousin to my father." He chuckled without humour. "I'm sure he'll have fun with her, like he did with you. I'd hoped he would have taught you a lesson before he'd touched you, but I guess what he did helped in the end. You have always been too weak to stand up for yourself."

"You motherfucker," I hissed. "You knew what he'd do to me,"

I spat in his face. He punched me in the stomach. I would have doubled over but his arm came across my chest holding me to the wall.

"Of course I did. I was the one to offer you up to him in the first place so he'd give me my first million."

"You sick fucking bastard," I coughed. Gaining control over my ragged breath, I leaned my head back against the wall and laughed dryly. "I guess, now you can say that I'm finally standing up for myself, Daddy dearest. You have no control over me anymore. I won't allow it." I glared at him. "My aunt and cousin are safe. I no longer have to play your games, old man. So you can fuck right off out of here." I brought up my fist and punched him in the face; his nose crunched under it. A satisfied smile filled my lips, only to be wiped away when my hand started screaming in pain.

Fuck. Had I broken it?

I didn't have time to worry about it. My eyes widened just before Dad backhanded me, and my head banged into the wall.

"That's where you're wrong." He grabbed my jaw in a tight unyielding grip and turned my face to him. "I will always have control, Julian. Always."

Fight.

And I did. I tried the best I could, but I was never the fighter, always the lover, and I was already in so much pain from the recent hits. I got a good few in before I slumped to the floor.

I collapsed and through tears, through the pain, through the agony, I watched and felt my father beat me senseless.

What surprised me was eventually, after so many seconds, minutes, hours—I wasn't sure—I stopped feeling.

My only thought was Mattie, my poppet.

Maybe that was what kept me alive after my father left.

Somehow, I stayed conscious enough to drag my beaten body to my phone and call the emergency services.

However, before I managed it, I watched through lifeless eyes as my father—the man who was supposed to be there for me, teach me, help me—smiled down at me and then walked, while whistling, out of my apartment, never looking back.

Probably hoping I'd die.

MATTIE

"Mum," I called, walking down the hallway from my bedroom. "I'm going to head over to Julian's," I added as I made it into the living room before my mobile started to ring.

"Oh, make sure you give him a big kiss from me," Mum said as she came into the living room from the kitchen wiping her hands.

After I sent her an eye roll, I said, "Sure, Mum." And then I answered my phone to a number I didn't know. "Hello?"

"Mattie, it's Melissa...Mattie, oh, God, Mattie. Julian's in the hospital. He's been beaten." Her voice cracked. "It...it doesn't look good, Mattie."

My blood drained from my body, the phone slipped from my hand and dropped to the floor.

"Matthew," Mum yelled. "Honey, what is it?" She was in my face, but I couldn't say anything. "Rich," Mum yelled. "RICH," she screamed. She must have picked up the phone because in the distance, I heard, "Hello, who is this...oh, no. Oh, my God."

Julian. Beaten.

No. Jesus. No.

Who would do such a thing?

Christ. My man, my boyfriend, had been beaten and it didn't look good.

What...?

No, I need him.

He…he couldn't leave me.

"Matthew," Dad barked in my face. "Let's go, son. We're going to the hospital." He took my arm in his hand and started for the front door. "Nancy, grab your bag, honey. Let's get to Julian."

"Yes, yes. Of course," Mum muttered.

"Mum." I swallowed back the sob fighting to get out.

"Yes, Mattie?'

"Someone beat him enough for Melissa to say it wasn't good." I paused. "Mum." My bottom lip trembled; tears filled my eyes. "He isn't good…I can't…fuck, he isn't good," I whispered.

"He'll be fine, honey. He's a fighter. He'll be fine," she said, but she didn't sound sure. My mum was always sure.

Fear ran through my body.

Fear rode with us until we arrived at the hospital.

And it stayed with me in the elevator to floor 5.

If I was honest with myself, fear stayed with me until I saw Melissa and she took my hand, told me he was unconscious, that the next twenty-four hours were crucial. There was swelling on his brain, internal bleeding and four cracked ribs, add the cuts, bruises and blood that coated some of his body… it was bad. So the fear stayed with me as she led me to Julian's room. It stayed with me when I walked in.

Then it fled.

Fear fled my body.

What replaced it was fury.

"Who did that to him?"

"Mattie, I…"

"Who?" I yelled.

"Shh, they will kick you out."

"I will not ask again after this, Melissa. Who did that to Julian?"

She sighed. "His father."

"What?" I growled low, menacingly.

"I told you he's never had a good relationship with his dad, his mum either. Twice before I've heard his father at Julian's apartment and when I've seen Julian after, he's had a black eye or a cut lip."

Holy shit, when Julian had come into football practice bruised, his father had done that to him...his fucking father.

"He abuses him, Mattie. He's had control over him for a long time, but Julian just fucked that up by doing something—"

"What?"

"It's not my place to say," she replied quietly.

"Melissa, I understand you don't want to tell me, but I *need* to know."

"His dad was going to send Julian's cousin to his father's, Julian's grandfather, if Julian didn't stay in the job he got him."

"What's so wrong with that?"

"Mattie," Melissa croaked. She licked her lips and looked to Julian, unshed tears in her eyes. "His father sent Julian there when he was young." She looked back to me, sorrow obvious in her eyes. "Julian's grandfather beat and raped him, Mattie."

My hand went to my stomach. I was going to be sick.

Fuck!

FUCK!

"No." I heard sobbed behind me. Melissa and I both turned to see my parents standing there. Dad had his arms wrapped around Mum's shoulders. They'd heard it all and by looking at it, Dad was feeling ill, yet fuming like I was.

Clenching my jaw, I hissed out, "Are you certain it was his father this time, Melissa?"

She sniffed and nodded. "Yes, I saw him leave. I raced up to Julian and...I found him on the floor, his phone near his hand.

He'd managed to call for help. I stayed on the phone until they arrived."

Looking from Melissa, I turned to my Dad. He gave me a chin lift, which was the answer I needed. "Mum, stay with Julian and Melissa. Dad—"

"No, son, I'm coming with you."

CHAPTER ELEVEN

MATTIE

*M*elissa gave us an address and Mum sent us on our way with a kiss, telling me she would pray for my man and never leave his side while I took care of business.

Why couldn't Julian's parents be like mine?

I would never understand how there could even be parents who treated their child with nothing but hate. It disgusted me, and to find out Julian had suffered through his whole life with parents like his, caused deep grief inside me.

His father needed to hurt for what he did to his son.

He needed to suffer like he'd made his son suffer.

He needed to feel pain like his son had.

"Dad—"

"Don't even say or think about it. I am coming with you, no one deserves…fuck, Matt, fuck. A father should never lay a hand on their child. A father…he needs to pay for this and something tells me the police won't be enough." The disgust in his voice was noticeable.

"Will we be enough?"

Dad actually smiled. "Yeah, kid, we will."

Good.

Silence filled the car, our own thoughts probably different to each other's. I just wanted to get the shit over with...then again, I wanted to drag it out, make Julian's father pay slowly...but what I wanted the most was to get back to my man. I wanted to be there when he woke, which he would. He had to and when he did, I didn't want him to live in fear. I didn't want him to feel dread or anxiety.

I wanted all his pain, all his concerns to go away and I was going to make it happen.

We pulled into a long gravel driveway, which led us up to a three-story brick home. Everything about it screamed money; everything about it screamed control. There were a few cars parked out the front. Dad pulled in beside some rich sporty car. I climbed out, walked to the front of the car and waited for Dad. When he joined me, he whistled low. "Like I was saying, cops won't do any good. It's fuckin' obvious he'd just buy them off."

Nodding, I started for the front door and rang the bell. My hands opened and closed at my sides, my heartrate picked up, only it wasn't from nerves. No, adrenaline was being pumped into my body.

"We get in there, get him into a room without witnesses and then we'll have a chat," Dad whispered.

"I get first chat," I growled low just as the front door opened.

In the doorway stood a man in his late fifties. He wore slacks, a dress shirt and jacket over it. He was home, yet he was still dressed as though he was going out to dine. A smirk touched my lips when I saw his nose was swollen. Julian had fought back.

That's my man. Pride filled me.

"Can I help you?" he asked, his tone snotty. He looked from Dad to me and back again. His broken nose raised in the air like he could smell something bad. Behind him, a woman passed by. She looked out to us and swiftly away, dismissing us to be nothing.

"Evenin', I wondered if we could have a private word with you?" Dad asked.

"I'm sorry, but I have my family visiting tonight. Can I ask what this is about?"

"Your son," I sneered.

"In that case, I'd really rather not talk to you at all. My son and I don't see eye to eye," he said.

I stepped up. He quickly backed up inside the house. "This really can't wait and won't take long, a quick word in your... office maybe?"

"Like I said—"

"Listen, Mr Jacob, if you don't talk to us, you'll soon find a reporter at your doorstep asking questions about why you sent your son to your father," Dad barked and stepped up behind me.

"You, I, this is uncalled for," he stuttered, turned and then walked off to the right. We followed him to the first door. He opened it, stepped in and walked around to the back of his desk.

Dad went in first. As I entered, I quickly closed the door behind me and locked it. Mr Jacob must have heard the lock click into place as his eyes widened.

"What do you want? Money to keep your mouths shut, not that there is anything the reporter can prove. Whatever Julian has told you is all a lie. As far as we are concerned, he went to his grandfather's because he was being a troublemaker. Still, I'm willing to keep you both silent." He bent over his desk, flicked his cheque book open, and snapped a pen off his desk. He looked up at us and said, "Well? How much?"

Walking around Dad, I kept going. I made it to the side of his desk before he straightened up and took a step back.

"I don't want anything from you. All I want is for you to leave my boyfriend alone," I ordered in a menacing voice.

His upper lip rose. "You're one of *them*." He straightened and glared at me. "You need to leave the premises immediately."

My dad snorted. I shook my head at Mr Jacob. "Yeah, I don't think so and if what you meant by *I'm one of them*, then yes, I'm gay. I am also very protective of my man. Which means…" I took the last step to where I was only inches from my target and then snarled, "I really don't like to see *my man* lying in a hospital bed right now. Especially finding out it was his own fucking father who put him there."

"You—"

"No, you need to shut the fuck up and listen to me." My hand went to his throat and I pushed him against the wall. "You will leave Julian alone. You will never see him again. You will never try to make contact in any way, shape, or form. You will also leave his aunt and cousin alone. If you try to look for them, I will know. If you try to exact any type of revenge, I won't be fucking happy, and when I'm not happy, things don't go down well. And they won't go down well when I ring the police and the media. And I will *out* all of you and your sick-as-fuck family for what they really are."

"You have no right—" he hissed.

Tightening my grip around his neck, I brought him forward and then slammed him back against the wall. Loosening my hold, I pulled my arm away so he would listen and concentrate on what I had to say. "Bullshit. I have every right when I want Julian to be safe. I want nothing…or anyone upsetting him again. If I find out you have, I'll fucking be back to make sure you get my message."

Dad cleared his throat. "Son, I think he's got the message."

Dad gestured lower on Mr Jacob. I looked down to see a wet patch.

Scoffing, I added. "It's you who's disgusting. It's people like you that the world would be better off without." Without another thought, only revenge, I raised my fist and planted it in his jaw. He doubled over. I lifted my knee and delivered it into his stomach. He coughed, and when he landed on his knees, I sent a kick to his side.

Nothing I was doing felt enough. He wasn't in enough pain.

Raising my fist once again, my dad's voice stopped me. "Son, enough." Dad grabbed my wrist before it could land. He brought me back a step, away from the pathetic, snivelling Mr Jacob.

"If my son hasn't got the message across now, then you'd be goddamn thick. You need to stay away from Julian, his aunt and cousin. What also needs to happen is that your fucked-up father is to be told he'll be watched. Now, I know you won't call the cops about what happened here, because if you do, everything will be out in the open. Have we made ourselves clear?" Dad asked coldly, standing with his arms folded across his chest.

Shrugging off his hold, I stalked to the door in his office. I waited for his answer with my hand on the handle. If I stayed near him or in there any longer, I wouldn't be responsible for what I did. But I needed his answer.

"Yes," he whispered. "I understand it all."

"Good," Dad said and then added, "Watch your back."

Opening the door, a woman gasped in fright. She had been at the door the whole time listening in. When I spotted her eyes, I knew exactly who she was. "How could you let that happen to your son?"

She blushed, her eyes diverted to the ground, only to snap back to me, her spine straightened out and her face hardened. "He's not worth the worry," she said, her voice devoid of emotion.

My upper lip rose. She was as bad as her husband was. However, what made her worse was that she was only doing it to protect herself from the man she married.

"Seems you heard everything. I want the same from you. You will never see your son again. You understand that?"

"Yes."

"Good. He deserves so much more than this fucked-up place. You will die old and lonely, and I can't wait for that day." With those parting words, words I knew cut her deep from the way she flinched, I stalked to the front door, hearing Dad's loud footsteps following me.

We said nothing as we climbed into the car and drove away. There was so much I was feeling, so much I wanted to say, only I couldn't. Everything was too overwhelming. The car pulled to the side of the road. Dad's hand appeared on the back of my neck. Forcing me forward, he ordered, "Just breathe, Matt. Calm down, kid, and breathe."

I did. With my head down, I took big gulps of air followed by a sob, which tore from my throat.

"It's okay, mate. You'll be okay. So fuckin' proud of you back there, son. So proud. You handled it and did a good job of it."

"I-it's not enough, Dad. I want him dead," I snapped, shrugging off his hand and sitting up, wiping my face clear.

"You've done all you can for Julian. You were Goddamn brilliant, Matthew. Wish I had recorded it for the boys."

Snorting to myself, I thought, *Yeah, his army mates would have liked it.*

Fuck.

"Julian has no family," I hissed. Except, maybe his aunt, but I felt she wasn't enough for my man.

"Wrong, he does. He has you *and* us."

Tears threatened again. "What happens if…"

Knowing what I was about to say, Dad barked, "It won't. A man knows when he finds the one he's supposed to spend the rest of his life with. You feel it deep down on first sight and then that spreads throughout your body, until that feeling consumes you."

Nodding, I thought that over and realised Dad was right. That was exactly what happened when I first met Julian.

I wanted him in my life forever. I wanted him protected, yet a part of me still thought I'd failed him. "That...man needs to hurt more."

"He will. Don't worry, he will. I'll get some guys to look into him. I'm fuckin' sure he ain't dealing in the straight and narrow. He's criminal in more ways than one; they'll find it and they'll deal with him. For now, you've done what you can and you did it fantastically. Now, let's get back to Julian. He'll want you there when he wakes, kid. No doubt if you're not, he'll scream the hospital down."

For the first time that night, I smiled. "Yeah, let's go."

FOUR DAYS LATER

JULIAN

When I woke, I expected to find myself lying on my living room floor. But the bright lights above me, and the noises from a machine beside me, let me know somehow I had been saved. A rough memory flooded into me, of doctors trying to get me to wake and telling me what happened.

Had that been recent? I wasn't sure.

Licking my dry lips, I turned my head to the hairy lump on

my bed beside my hand. I slowly reached out and ran my fingers through silky hair.

Mattie bolted upright, his red, sleep-deprived eyes wide with worry. "Julian?"

"Hey, poppet." I smiled.

He stood quickly and reached for the cup on the table beside my bed. He leaned over and held a straw to my parched lips. I sucked back the water, wishing I was well enough to suck back something else, something that was connected to Mattie, but I couldn't. My body ached all over.

Mattie took the cup away and I sighed, resting back into the bed. I looked up at my toy-boy. Oh, God, he had tears in his beautiful eyes. What the doctors said had been true... frightening my man.

My man leaned over again and touched his forehead against mine gently. "I nearly lost you."

"Poppet." Tears formed in my own eyes. Reaching up, which caused my cracked ribs to pinch, still I kept going, rubbing down his back. I wanted to reassure my man. "I'm still here. You can't get rid of me that easily."

"Fuck, Julian," he choked. Wetness touched my shoulder, soaking straight through the thin hospital gown. "I nearly lost you."

Oh, snap off a strap on. My man was hurting.

Cupping his jaw, I brought his face up to mine and touched my sore lips to his. "I must have bad breath, but you'll have to suffer through it. I'm fine, honey. I'm alive and I'll keep surviving."

"You will." He nodded. His eyes turned hard. "You'll never see him again, Julian. He will not harm you. He'll not come near you."

My eyes widened. "H-how do you know?"

"Doesn't matter how I know, babe. I took care of it. Your

family is, from now on, dead to you. They won't cause any shit for you, your aunt or your cousin. Instead, you have a new family, a better one. One who will love, care and cherish you. You have us, me and my family."

A sob took hold and bubbled over. My hands covered my face as I cried.

No one.

No one had ever protected me.

No one had cared so much to want to stop my pain.

To stop the man who'd made my life hell.

Until Matthew Alexander.

Until, my man, my toy-boy and poppet.

He was giving me a gift so precious, only I didn't know how to show what it meant to me.

He was giving himself and his family to me, to a man who had been lonely, hiding behind humour for so long.

Now I could survive and live, and feel loved.

"Julian, baby?"

Wiping my face, I looked up at him and asked, "You really… you took…you…he won't bother me again?"

He nodded. "No, never."

"Well then, can I just say…you're stuck with me now, and even if you tried to leave, I'll follow you," he promised.

"Fuck, I hope so."

THREE WEEKS LATER

It was my last day as a masseur in the football club. Once discharged from hospital, a week and a half earlier, I gave my notice. Coach asked me to do one last session while they interviewed possible replacements. I was fine with it, Mattie not so much. My hero was possessive and demanding since I'd been in hospital. I never thought I would see him like that when it came to me, but I had and I liked it a lot. I liked it more than chocolate and *that* I could live off for the rest of my gay life. Things had changed. I had a new addiction and his name was Mattie.

He didn't want me to go to the last job at the football centre because he didn't want me to exhaust myself, even though I was pretty much healed, only bruises showed. I doubted that was the only case. He still let me flirt, that was impossible for me to stop, but he didn't like me touching other men.

So when my last client had been done, I was shocked when I walked out of the room to see Mattie striding in and toward me. The other team players were still around for a meeting. Mattie was no longer a part of the team though since he quit.

My eyes widened when he stopped in front of me, smiled, and then winked.

"W-what are you doing here?" I whispered.

"Hey, Alexander," Jackson called, the biggest prick of them all. "What you doin' here? Come crawling back to the team? Sorry you lost all the footy hype, all the pussy that comes along with it?"

So my man wouldn't feel as though he was on the spot with me standing there, I started to slide behind him for an escape. However, he reached his hand out and snagged my wrist.

"Nope." He grinned at the players. "I just came to pick up my boyfriend."

Holy butt plugs.

Did he just say that aloud?

He called me his boyfriend...in front of people.

I wasn't hearing things, right?

"You're...you...and him?" Jackson stuttered.

"Yeah," Mattie said, he looked to me, gave me a quick kiss on the lips and then added, "Julian's amazing in the bedroom and out."

A deep chuckle filled the quiet room. I looked with shocked eyes to see Lions laughing, bent over holding his stomach. He stood and said, "Good on ya, man."

"That's sick," Jackson sneered.

Mattie tensed. "I don't give a fuck what you think, Jackson, or anyone in here for that matter. I'm happy with who I am. Those who don't like it can get fucked."

Oh, my brave, brave man.

He said nothing else; instead, he slid his hand into mine and led me from the changing rooms. He walked my stunned body to his car. I had wondered why he wanted to drop me off that night, now I knew.

He wanted to show who he was.

He wanted to show that I meant something to him.

That had been the best 'coming out' I had ever seen.

Suddenly, my body was twisted and I was pushed up against his car. He got up in my personal space and growled, "If we didn't have an audience, I would fuck you against my car here and now."

My balls flew up to my stomach.

I had an aching need to come.

"Well then, poppet, we'd better get home."

And I meant home. To *our* apartment. Where he had moved himself in after the incident and hadn't left.

The drive home was quiet. For once, I was at a loss for what to say because I had so much to say.

As soon as we were in the door, I was once again pushed up against something, that time the door after Mattie kicked it closed. "Naked, now," he ordered and I would have complied if he hadn't shoved his tongue in my mouth. I groaned around his attack and thrust my hard dick into his.

"Jesus," he hissed, taking his lips from mine, which I wasn't happy about. He saw it and chuckled. "Go and get naked, lie on the bed and be ready for me, Julian. I need a moment before I come in."

"Why?" I asked.

"So I can take you without hurting you. Because right now, all I can think about is sliding my cock into your arse. We need lube and that's in the bedroom. Get. Ready. For. Me. Now."

"Right-ho, captain." I smiled and then ran to the bedroom.

By the time my man walked in, I was naked and lying on my back on the bed. His eyes darkened when he saw me. He licked his lower lip and bit down, quickly undressing. When he climbed onto the bed at the bottom, he took hold of my ankles and slowly separated my legs. Kissing my fevered skin at my thighs, he made his way up to my hip where he bit down, causing me to gasp. He travelled higher to my stomach, bypassing the main area that wanted, *needed* attention. My cock grumbled in displeasure. But my heart beat faster as his lips kissed all the way up my chest, my neck, my cheek, and then finally, they claimed my mouth in a wet, heated kiss.

He pulled back, his arms tense and he clutched the sheets on the bed beside my head while he looked down at me. "Are you all ready for me?" he growled.

Speechless, which was a significant event on its own, I nodded, knowing he was asking if I was lubed and ready for the taking.

"Good," he said.

The intense look in his eyes was impossible to glance away from, so as he, with one hand, spread my legs that little bit further, I watched his jaw clench when he positioned himself at my entrance. With his hand on my thigh, he brought it high, gripped it harder, and slowly, he pushed inside of me.

My back arched. I loved the feeling of Mattie filling me, and watching his face as he did it was even better. Once he was all the way in, he took hold of my jaw and ran a thumb over my bottom lip. "You're mine."

"Yes," I whispered.

"You love me?"

Oh. God.

"Yes."

"Good, because I love you." He slid nearly all the way out of me and forced his way back in fast. Both of us groaned. Our bodies made love to each other. It was deliciously slow and hotter than it had ever been before.

"You always feel so good," Mattie growled, flattening his body to mine, but still keeping all his weight off me. "You better not come. You've got to take me," he demanded. Which was impossible. As he slid in and out of me, his body rubbed against my hard dick, making the friction enough to set me off.

"Too late," I panted. "I'm about to—"

"You wait for me, Julian," my man ordered.

"I...can't..."

"Fuck, yes, you wait. I'm nearly there."

My hands wrapped around his waist, bringing his weight down on me more, so there was more pressure from his body on my throbbing cock.

"Poppet," I hissed.

He knew.

"Yes, baby. Come now." He cried out as his cock pulsated inside me, spreading his warm cum in my arse. Immediately after, I exploded all over my stomach and his.

His head came to rest on my shoulder, our breathing erratic.

"Love you, poppet."

"Love you more, my Julian."

EPILOGUE

FOUR YEARS LATER.

MATTIE

For four years, the person who claimed the other half of my soul has been cemented in my life. Four blissful years. Of course, like any couple, we'd had our ups and downs. One day was when my world was tipped upside down when the police turned up at our apartment—three years earlier —and said my parents died in a car accident, which had been a lie. Julian was my rock. He'd kept me functioning every day. He was the one who told me to find my sister, after we'd buried them. Or at the time what we thought was them. Even though I was reluctant to, because I knew her ex was cruel and cunning, I thought I could get away with it and find her without an incident.

Unfortunately, I did all of it without informing Julian. As for the why I didn't tell him, it was simple. I wanted him to stay safe. There were too many risks in finding Zara. However, he followed me, like he promised a year earlier. My man came for me. He wasn't happy to have been left behind and I couldn't blame him, even if that trouble nearly had him shot alongside of me. Still, to recent days, he never once regretted what he did. He never regretted coming to find me, and no matter the issues we'd had over the years, I also never regretted the day he walked... well, was dragged through Zara's front door. If he hadn't, I wouldn't be where I was. I wouldn't be opening my own real estate agency. I wouldn't have my family, and his, surrounding me, and I wouldn't have had the love that filled me each day when I saw Julian, or when I woke up with him, when I watched him smile, laugh and joke.

He was my world.

Which was why I was about to make it final.

"You ready to do this?" Zara, my sister, asked.

Looking up into the mirror in her bathroom, I shook my head. "What if I was still taking a piss?"

"Pfft, like you were. You needed to come in here to splash water on your face to compose yourself."

She knew me too well. "I wish Josie were here for this," I said sadly as I dried my hands. Josie was our foster sister. Not that we saw her as anything but blood. Unfortunately, she was at university in Melbourne.

Zara nodded and moved out of the doorway so I could slip out. "I know, so do I. We can hope she comes home for the Easter holidays."

I doubted it. She hadn't been home in a long time. She had me worried actually.

"So..." Zara trailed off.

Shit. I knew that *so* was going to be bad.

"Everyone's arrived, just waiting on the man himself."

Suddenly, I stopped, spun at my sister and glared. "What do you mean by everyone? I said family only."

She rolled her eyes. "And I meant family, the *family* is here." She bit her bottom lip, telling me she was lying.

We walked out into their large living room, which Talon had extended out after their twins were born, to see there were a lot more than just family there.

"Jesus, Zara," I hissed.

She placed her arm around my shoulders and said, "Julian will love the show and besides, they're all family. They're Talon's biker brethren."

Yes, not only were our parents there, but half the biker club Talon was the president of were as well. Which actually surprised me. It surprised me because I didn't think they'd want to be a part of the day's event. However, I was also warmed how they'd accepted Julian and myself in their lives when they were, as Zara and her pussy posse would call them, bad-arse mother-fuckers.

Talon found my eyes and sent me a chin lift. I returned it. Two years ago, when the others found out what Julian had been through, what I had rescued him from, Talon came to me with a question. It had been a year after Zara's hell when Dad informed me that Julian's pain was gone in more ways than one. Sweet victory had been delivered. Julian's father was heading to prison for fraud and his mother, with nothing left, took it badly, so badly she was in the psych ward.

So when Talon came to me and asked me if I wanted Julian's father gone, I thought long and hard about it. In the end, I decided to let him live his misery longer than what death would bring.

Not one to keep anything from my man, I told Julian all about it. His reply was that I picked well.

"He's here," Mum suddenly screamed.

Everyone quickly made a beeline for other rooms, hiding while my man walked up to the front door. I called him earlier when he was working with the girls at Talon's strip club, teaching them dance moves. I would never have guessed he'd have that job, but he loved it, and I was happy with whatever he wanted to do. So I'd called him and told him Zara was putting together a dinner; she wanted our help in preparing it, and in return, we'd get a free meal.

Julian, never one to knock back a meal from my sister or time to spend with our nieces and nephews, he asked no questions and said he'd be there.

Before Zara ran to the kitchen, she gave me a quick kiss and said, "You'll be fine."

Hell. I hoped so.

When I heard him turn the handle, I got down to one knee. He swung open the door, his lips parted, ready to announce he was there. Instead, he stopped and froze. His eyes filled with tears as he watched me.

"Julian Jacob, from the moment I saw you, I knew you would change my life. I knew you were it for me. I was hiding in many ways, but it was your light that shined through, that gave me courage to be the person I am today. I could never imagine my life without you in it. You're the other half of my soul. You're my forever and I can't wait to see where our future will lead us...as long as we're together. I love you more than anything, my own life included, Julian. Will you marry me?"

A whimper escaped his lips as they quivered. Tears fell freely from his eyes, his hand went to his chest and finally...

Finally, my man put me at ease.

He nodded.

"Yes, yes, yes, a million times yes," he cried, ran to me and dropped to his knees, wrapping me up in his warm embrace after I placed a ring on his finger.

People clapped and screamed around us. Julian cried harder.

Bring on the future, because I have my man. I have my life, my soul at my side.

JULIAN

Here I thought it was going to be a day like every other. I was wrong, so wrong. When those words from my better half crawled out of his mouth and surrounded me like a warm blanket, I swear my pounding gay heart stopped. I swear I had gone insane and was imagining the whole scene.

When I didn't come to my senses, I realised it was true.

The sight before me was real.

My man.

My brave, sweet, possessive, strong, gorgeous man was on his knee in front of me and proposing.

My life couldn't get any better.

My life was perfect.

I had my man. I had a family who loved me no matter how I acted. A new job I loved because I got to groove it out all day and most of all, I woke up each day knowing that none of it was a dream. It was all reality and it was wonderful.

As I cried in my man's arms, people... no our family, clapped, laughed and cheered around us, I felt a tug on my sleeve. Turning my head to the side, I saw a beaming Maya standing there.

"You're *really* my uncle now." She giggled. "Yay."

My arm surrounded her and I brought her to our chests. "I sure am, pumpkin pie." I smiled and kissed her forehead.

She pulled back to meet my eyes. "Do you know what would be even better?"

"What?"

"If you had a baby yourself. You and Uncle Mattie are so awesome, you would be great daddies."

Biting my bottom lip to try and control myself from bursting into hysterics and scaring her, I nodded and kissed her cheek. "That would be nice," I said.

"Out," Talon barked. "Let's get this fucking engagement party started. Blue, start the grill out back. Nancy, you set the food up outside. Feed people, woman."

Mattie's lips touched my ear. I shivered. "There's something else I wanted to ask you." He lifted his head and said to his niece. "Maya, sweetie, can you go help your nanny?"

"Hell yeah," she yelled.

My hand went over my mouth to hide my laugh as my man helped me to stand.

"Talon," Zara barked as Maya skipped off. "Do you see what you have done to our child?"

"Relax, Kitten." Talon laughed. "Maya, don't say hell around your mum."

"Okay, Daddy. Sorry, Mum," she called back.

"Maya," Zara started to scold.

"I promise to not say hell in front of anyone but Daddy. I won't even say it at school."

Zara blinked and blinked again. She threw up her hands as Maya went through the back door. "I give in." She turned a glare to her husband. "You have to deal with it when the school calls."

"She knows the rules, Kitten. S'all good." He kissed his wife quickly and turned to us. "You gonna tell him or what?"

113

Turing to Mattie, I saw his eyes roll. "I'm going to ask him, not tell him."

"What's going on?" I asked.

Mattie took my hands in his. My heart had only just settled, but now it was taking off once again from the serious look upon my man's face. "Julian, Maya was right."

My head jutted back. "About what?"

"We'd make great parents..."

Tears formed in my eyes. I blinked them away and pulled a hand from Mattie's to cover my mouth. "What?" I uttered behind my hand.

"I'd like to have our own family and I know it's something you have always wanted. So I went to Zara and Talon, asking them if they could help."

Oh, God.

Goosebumps broke out all over my body. Tears fell from my eyes.

"What?" I whispered, and with a shaking hand, I rubbed my eyes, my hand soon falling over my stomach, as if that would control the butterflies.

Mattie squeezed the hand he still held. "Babe..."

Oh, God.

Tears pooled in his own eyes.

"Zara and Talon are offering us the chance to be dads."

A sob caught in my throat. I looked from Mattie to Zara. She was also crying. She nodded.

It was real.

It was happening.

"Really?" I cried.

"Yes," Mattie said softly, his emotions were raw and unhidden.

"I love you so very much, poppet." I managed before wrapping my arms around my man as the dam broke. I kissed him, hugged him and cried on him. All while he stood there and took it.

There was one thing I would be grateful for from my father and that was when he ordered me to do that job. If he hadn't, I wouldn't have found Matthew. I wouldn't have found my beautiful future.

SNEAK PEEK — THE SECRET'S OUT

HAWKS MC: CAROLINE SPRINGS CHARTER: BOOK 1

PREQUEL

NANCY

Nancy Alexander placed her phone on the table. She looked down, but wasn't really focused on it. No, her mind was running over things from the phone call she just had.

Her youngest daughter, Josie, hadn't been home that Christmas holiday. In fact, she hadn't returned home in a long time and Nancy was worried.

For the tenth time that day, she called her daughter's mobile demanding answers.

Only it wasn't her daughter who supplied them.

Josie's housemate, where she lived in a small apartment close to her school, had answered.

"Mrs Alexander?" she whispered into the phone. Nancy should have realised then that something was wrong, but she didn't.

"Simone, honey, how many times do I have to tell you to call me Nancy? Now, can you tell me where my daughter is? I'm getting sick of this run around. She's either too busy to talk or on her way out somewhere. But I'm worried about my girl, Simone."

"You should be," Simone uttered and Nancy started to panic.

Nancy sat straight in her chair. "Tell me, Simone."

"It's not really my place."

"No, Simone, you tell me now so I can help."

"She won't want her mum here. That'll make things worse."

"Simone, tell me!"

"Josie's in the bathroom, but I can hear her crying. She cries a lot, Nancy, and I think it has to do with some guys who are hassling her. She's so quiet and timid. The stupid-heads find it fun to cause her problems."

"Is that all?" Nancy snapped in a hard tone.

"I-I think so? Please, please don't come here. I swear it'll make things worse."

"Oh, I won't come, darling. I'll be sending someone else."

"Who?"

"Doesn't matter. Just know help will be arriving soon, and watch over my girl 'til then."

"I will, Mrs–I mean, Nancy."

"Thank you, Simone, for telling me."

"I hate seeing Josie upset."

"I do also. I'm going to let you go now. I need to make a phone call."

Simone hung up the phone and not long after, Nancy stared at the phone on the table thinking. She picked it back up again and put it to her ear.

"Hello, my wonderful son-in-law."

"Nancy," was all Talon said.

"Josie is having trouble as school. Some guys are... annoying her, Talon."

Usually, Nancy would taunt him to get a rise, but she wasn't in the mood, and she knew her son-in-law could tell by her tone.

"Fuck," Talon growled low. "I'll handle it."

"Good," Nancy said and hung up.

Chapter One

JOSIE

Life on my own wasn't what I thought it would be. Two years of living away from home was getting to me. Two years of independence, two years of finding myself was...hard. Harder than I pictured. Sure, I found myself...in a way. Sure, I had independence. I had a job, had a great friend, and a roof over my head. Still, all I wanted was to be home. Be with the family who had opened their arms wide for me. They had adopted me, regardless of how troubled I was. I missed my sister, Zara, my brother, Matthew, but especially my mum and dad. I even missed my brothers-in-law, the goofy one, Julian, and the sometimes scary one, Talon. Most of all, I missed my nieces and nephews. Their light had helped me through many dark times. They were young and didn't know the real world could be scary. It was their excitement over little things that I appreciated and missed.

Which was why I had stayed away from home so many times over the past two years, because if I went there, I knew I'd want to stay and never leave again. I'd want back in *their* world, their open arms and the protection they provided me each and every day. I'd want to be surrounded in it all once more and forever. Never leaving again.

However, I had to stay strong.

I wanted to prove to them, and especially myself, I was able to live in the real world, no matter how scared I was each day, or how my brain screamed at me to stop the ridiculousness and get home. And no matter how much I hated living through the taunting and teasing each day for the past year, my decision was resolute.

Since *they* found out I was petrified of most men, of human contact, it had all changed.

The first time it happened they enjoyed the reaction they got from me. They thrived on the fact that it unnerved me.

Since then, it happened all the time, just so they could see me cower and cringe.

I was lucky to have found Simone, the sweet girl with shoulder-length black hair and dark blue eyes. It was as though fortune had rained down on me when it was Simone who answered the same ad I had two years earlier. It was an ad in the local paper I'd found before I moved to Melbourne, for two house guests to look after a fully furnished home while the owner travelled for business. When the owner was home, we rarely saw him. He tended to stay in the master bedroom. He was quiet and kept to himself, like me.

The idea of living my life as the local cat lady or hermit had been promising, for the first few months after I had moved in, which was possibly why Simone took it upon herself to get me out and about. She was determined for me to start living my life the way an eighteen-year-old should after flying the nest.

She showed me there was hope, kindness and love in the world outside of my family.

Simone was a great friend, the best anyone could have, trusting, loyal and bubbly. She took me under her wing and showed me how to get drunk, do shots, and dance until my legs wanted to fall from my body, just so they could rest. Dancing was fun.

At least I had that one year respite at uni before my new hell started. Even then, I kept to my shy self, still forming the knowledge of how people went about their day, how they communicated in the different way I was with my family. If it weren't for Simone, I would have been on my own, and surviving would have been the wrong term.

Everything had been okay...until Cameron Peterson took an interest in me.

At first I thought he was different.

I thought he was nice.

I'd been wrong on so many levels.

To start off, he *had* been nice, sweet even. He saw that I was shy, but still he approached me slowly and with caution. He said kind things to me and didn't invade my comfort zone. But things must have been moving too slow for him, because after one weekend, a weekend where we saw each other out at a club, he changed.

He thought he owned me.

He thought I wanted him.

He had been wrong and he didn't like it.

The night we were out, he was drunk, and he was a mean drunk. I knew that because once he spotted me on the dance floor, he stalked over to me with a feral glint in his eyes, or so Simone explained afterwards when she watched his approach. His hands went straight to my waist. I flinched and tried to move away, but his grip tightened. My breath caught in my throat. For a moment, all but a second, I was scared it was David. The man who took so many things from me, but most of all, my innocence. Even though I knew the sudden thought was ridiculous as he was dead, I couldn't stop the fear seeping into my body. I stiffened as Cameron rubbed his arousal into my backside. Simone, sensing my fear, like she did every time, came forward and pushed Cameron back. I hadn't told Simone of my past; however, she only had to watch me, like any other, to see that I was new to physical contact from people I didn't know. She always did her best to steer people away from me, no matter the situation and slowly, she was teaching me not all contact was bad. Not when it came from people I knew and trusted, so when she hugged me, I only flinched a little when it would startle me. I turned to see Cameron sneer at Simone, until he noticed I was watching and changed his expression to a lusty, drunken smile.

"Hey, baby," he said.

I cringed. "I-I'm not your baby, Cameron."

"Sure you are." He reached for me again. I backed up a step, my hands out in front of me. "Don't be like that." He chuckled.

In a loud enough voice so he could hear me over the pumping music, I said, "I'd prefer it if you didn't touch me, please."

He rolled his eyes. "Don't be stupid, Jo-Jo, you know you want me. I see the way you look at me." Lightning fast, he reached out and snagged my wrist, dragging me forward so our chests collided.

"Don't. Please, don't, you're drunk. I'll talk to you tomorrow," I pleaded and tried to pry myself away. Simone stepped up next to us trying to get Cameron off me, but he wouldn't have it. They started yelling at each other.

Tears formed, and just as quickly, they rolled down my cheeks, leaving a wet trail behind. There was no way to stop the whirlwind of emotions wreaking havoc inside my body. Spotting my tears, Cameron wiped them away. Ignoring Simone, he leaned toward me to get my attention. "You want me, Jo-Jo, like all the girls do. No one says no to me." Then he slammed his lips down on mine. I struggled and fought against him, but nothing worked, so when he shoved his tongue inside my mouth, I bit him.

Pushed away by strong hands, I stumbled into Simone. She wrapped her arms around my waist to steady me. "You stupid jerk," Simone screamed. People started taking notice. I was surprised they hadn't beforehand, though most were drunk and in their own little worlds. Some looked too scared to say or do anything. I couldn't blame them. I would have been the same.

"You stupid bitch," he snarled at me. He wiped his mouth and studied me. Whatever he saw had him smirking. "You really hate it, don't you? Touching, attention. Here I thought you were just shy, but now I know you have mental problems." He chuckled. "Makes it more fun for me." He winked, turned, and walked away.

From that night on, he became my personal nightmare. I was terrified by his obsession with me.

He'd show up wherever I was. His eyes travelled along with every step I took. His smirk turned sexual and his words sinister. He wanted me, but he couldn't have me and he did not like that at all. So much so, if he couldn't make it to me, he'd have his friends do his job for him and they'd follow me. I could hear their fake whispered conversations of how strange I was. They'd call me names like tease, slut and ugly.

All I wanted was to be left alone.

However, they wouldn't. They were puppets following their master's lead.

Once, six months ago, I even tried to go on a date with a shy guy like me. I could tell he was nervous. He didn't even make a move to hold my hand, which I liked. It went well, until Cameron showed up at the café. He slid into the booth opposite me, next to my date, and told him that I was a cock tease, that I had problems, and was mentally unstable. He warned my date that if he continued to date me, I would turn into a stalker, like I had with him. Apparently, Cameron was just following the 'bro code'. All men had to stick together and warn each other of the freaks, like me.

Of course, because my date was worried it was true and the fact that he didn't want Cameron's attention, he fled the café and I never saw him again.

After that, Cameron went from standing back and teasing, to touching. Any chance he got, he would rub up against me, run his hand down my back. Pretend to lean in to kiss me or tap me on the shoulder and yell, "Boo." Again, if he couldn't be around to do it, he'd have his friends fill in for him.

Every day I was a nervous wreck.

I'd become a jittery fool, one who was even more timid and withdrawn than I'd been after Zara and Talon saved me from David.

I was losing hope in society once more. I knew Simone saw it. I knew she was worried for me, but there was nothing I could do. I couldn't go to the police. I didn't want the attention, and I knew Cameron would make my life worse than it already was.

My grades declined, and once more, my social skills took a hit. I was like a zombie walking around campus, with my head low, my books to my chest and a hunched posture, all while I waited for hell to begin for the day.

Even my boss, a fifty-year-old woman named Marybeth, noticed the change in me. I'd lost count of how many times she had asked me if I was okay. All I could do was nod. Thankfully, due to my 'shyness', she had taken me off floor duty, from serving customers. Instead, I was out back helping with the preparation of the food and washing the dishes. I loved her for it. She knew I struggled being around strangers. At first, she'd encouraged me to try floor duty and for a while there, I loved it because I didn't have to touch anyone and I only had to speak a few words...until everything went pear-shaped because of Cameron.

Misery was my name and I didn't know how to change it.

I wanted to reach out to my parents, my sister or brother even, but I didn't. Why? Because I felt I needed to deal with it on my own. It was my choice to move away. It was my choice to attend university, to be independent. So if I ran home, if I rang them crying about how terrible it all was, I would be a failure. I couldn't become *that* person. I needed to show, not only myself, but my family that I had grown. Their protection, their love had contributed to my freedom, my independence. I was no longer that little girl who was carried from a nightmare. At least, I didn't feel I was. No matter what I was enduring every day and no matter how much it hurt, strength grew inside of me.

Still, I missed my family with every fibre of my being, missed their warmth and protection.

Because of that, everything hurt.

Simone tried her best to make me happy, get me to laugh, and for her, I did as best as I could.

I knew that when I smiled or laughed at her jokes, it didn't show in my eyes. There was no fooling her either; she would see through my façade every time, causing her to sigh in defeat. But she never gave up. The next day, she would make another attempt. I loved her for trying so much.

I stopped doing anything other than classes or work. As soon as class or my shift finished, I would race home. I was lucky I didn't live far from both places.

Cameron showed up many times at home. If Simone was home, she'd send him away. If she wasn't, I'd sit on the floor in the corner of the living room to listen and wait until he eventually left. I'd never cave and open the door to him. If I did, the outcome wouldn't be pretty. His foul language and anger was enough to convince me he was a threat. It was that anger that would be taken out on me physically, destroying what little hope I had of ever finding normalcy.

About two months earlier his nightly visits finally stopped. One night when he came by, Parker, the owner, was home. He must have had a very bad business trip because when Cameron banged on the door, Parker swung my bedroom door open. The force from it hit my wall, causing me to squeal and jump. Parker stood in the doorway scowling. He then demanded to know if the loser at the door was annoying me. All I could do was nod. I was too terrified to do anything else. Once I answered, Parker then barked out, "Never be scared of me." I gave another nod and then he added, "I'll deal with it." He closed my door with a bang and stomped off toward the front door.

I wished I had the courage to have seen what occurred at the front door, but all I heard was yelling, mainly from Parker. After a few noises, which sounded like punches, things fell silent and Parker was at my door again opening it. "He won't come here again. If he troubles you at other places, you need to find someone to deal with it." With that, he closed my door, gently that time, and went back to his room, leaving me with yet more questions regarding my housemate. All I knew was that he looked to be around twenty-four, and he travelled a lot; though I wasn't sure he liked what he did.

If it wasn't for the day he handled Cameron, I would have kept on thinking he was a nerdy bookworm with how he stayed locked in his room reading with his sexy glasses on his nose. I had seen he was a fan of reading when one day I'd been walking past his room, his door suddenly opened and he stepped out. I looked over his shoulder quickly to see his walls were lined with bookcases and *many* books sat upon them. However, the way he handled my trouble at the front door had me second guessing myself. Parker had been true to his word though. Cameron never darkened our doorstep again. Though, it hadn't changed the attention I still got at uni. If anything, whatever Parker did caused Cameron's stare to turn deadly.

After that incident, Parker stayed around for two more days before he left again. We said nothing to each other about what had happened. Even when he returned two weeks later to stay another three nights, zilch was shared between us. Since then, he hadn't been back. I couldn't help but pray he was okay.

Simone, knowing something had changed, asked me why Cameron wasn't coming to the house any longer. I told her about Parker. Her eyes glazed over and she got a small, satisfied smile on her face. "Now we just need to find someone to do whatever he did in public when dickface is still screwing with you," she'd said.

Standing in the bathroom, I shook all thoughts from my mind, my eyes were still red from crying in the shower. I waited in the bathroom trying to hide it from Simone. I took a deep breath and swiped at the fogged-up mirror to stare at my reflection.

I'd lost weight, enough for me to know that I was underweight. My cheek bones jutted out and my once shiny styled hair looked lifeless, so did the bags under my eyes. I lifted my red waves and let them fall back into the wet mess it was. Simone had surprised me on my twentieth birthday, just four months earlier, with a beauty day.

I'd been reluctant to go due to my phobias. Still, because Simone was such a great supportive friend, I sucked it up for the day and went out with her to get my nails painted black and my long, very curly, red hair was styled into a modern wave. Something I absolutely loved. It was too bad it looked lifeless once again, even when dried. What didn't help was my lack of care.

My mum had been ecstatic when I sent her a picture of my hair. She'd gushed over it and told me how beautiful I was.

God, I missed her.

People were right. Home was where the heart is, because mine had never left Ballarat. My heart stayed with my family, only making an appearance sometimes when Simone brought it out in me. Any other day I was lifeless, a shell.

Maybe I was being overly dramatic, maybe I could go home and not think I was a failure.

Honestly, I didn't know what to do.

I didn't know because I stopped thinking a while ago.

I stopped feeling.

All that mattered were the grades I needed.

At least there was still that tiny, minute spark inside of me that wanted the future career I longed for so long ago.

Currently, that was the only thing that kept me there, that kept me from running back to my family.

I often wondered if I had someone to care for me back then, maybe I would have noticed David's attention was more than fatherly. Perhaps I would have seen that he was nothing more than a dirty old man lusting for a minor. If someone had been there for me, I wouldn't have been beaten, broken or raped.

I wasn't stupid. I knew I couldn't help all children being abused or taken advantage of by becoming a social worker. But I could help some and I would fight with everything I had to make sure those children knew *they were worth something*. Those children needed to know life could get better and I would do anything in my power to make that happen for them.

So for now, I would hold onto that little spark inside of me for those children.

I would get the grades I needed and continue each day as it came.

I would do all that and then, finally, before I took any job with children, I would take the time to sort myself out. No past, no hurt, no pain of my own would reflect on any case I took on.

For now, I would continue to pray and hope that each day may be better than the last.

ACKNOWLEDGEMENTS

As always a huge thank you to Becky and her team at Hot Tree Editing.

To everyone who LOVES Julian and Mattie as much as I do and wanted their story. My Hawks' world wouldn't have lived if it wasn't for you reading them!

ALSO BY LILA ROSE

Hawks MC: Ballarat Charter

Holding Out (FREE) Zara and Talon

Climbing Out: Griz and Deanna

Finding Out (novella) Killer and Ivy

Black Out: Blue and Clarinda

No Way Out: Stoke and Malinda

Coming Out (novella) Mattie and Julia

Hawks MC: Caroline Springs Charter

The Secret's Out: Pick, Billy and Josie

Hiding Out: Dodge and Willow

Down and Out: Dive and Mena

Living Without: Vicious and Nary

Walkout (novella) Dallas and Melissa

Hear Me Out: Beast and Knife

Breakout (novella) Handle and Della

Fallout: Fang and Poppy

Standalones related to the Hawks MC

Out of the Blue (Lan, Easton, and Parker's story)

Out Gamed (novella) (Nancy and Gamer's story)

Outplayed (novella) (Violet and Travis's story)

Romantic comedies

Making Changes

Making Sense

Fumbled Love

Trinity Love Series

Left to Chance

Love of Liberty (novella)

Paranormal

Death (with Justine Littleton)

In The Dark

CONNECT WITH LILA ROSE

Webpage: www.lilarosebooks.com

Facebook: http://bit.ly/2du0taO

Instagram: www.instagram.com/lilarose78/

Goodreads:
www.goodreads.com/author/show/7236200.Lila_Rose